The Invasion

Nancy Rue

PUBLISHING
Colorado Springs, Colorado

THE INVASION
Copyright © 1997 by Nancy N. Rue
All rights reserved. International copyright secured.

Library of Congress Cataloging-in-Publication Data
Rue, Nancy N.
  The invasion / Nancy Rue.
      p.   cm.—(Christian heritage series ; 11)
  Summary: When British soldiers plunder his family's plantation near Williamsburg
and the overseer hired by his father proves to be dishonest, eleven-year-old Thomas takes
matters into his own hands.

    ISBN 1-56179-541-0
    [1. Fathers and sons—fiction.   2. Williamsburg (Va.)—History—Revolution, 1775-
1783—Fiction. 3. United States—History—Revolution, 1775-1783—Fiction. 4. Christian
Life—Fiction.] I. Title. II. Series: Rue, Nancy N. Christian heritage series; bk. 11.
PZ7.R85515In   1997
[Fic]—dc21   97-5400
                                                                                       CIP
                                                                                        AC

Published by Focus on the Family Publishing,
Colorado Springs, Colorado 80995.
Distributed in the U.S.A. and Canada by Word Books, Dallas, Texas.

This author is represented by the literary agency of Alive Communications, 1465 Kelly
Johnson Blvd., Suite 320, Colorado Springs, CO 80920.

Focus on the Family books are available at special quantity discounts when purchased in
bulk by corporations, organizations, churches, or groups. Special imprints, messages, or
excerpts can be produced to meet your needs. For more information, write: Special Sales,
Focus on the Family Publishing, 8605 Explorer Dr., Colorado Springs, CO 80920; or call
(719) 531-3400 and ask for the Special Sales Department.

This is a work of fiction, and any resemblance between the characters in this book and
real persons is coincidental.

Editor: Keith Wall
Cover Design: Bradley Lind
Cover Illustration: Cheri Bladholm

Printed in the United States of America

97 98 99 00/10 9 8 7 6 5 4 3 2 1

*For Richard Douthat,
an important bridge in our family*

Chapter One

"Remember what I told you," Malcolm Donaldson whispered into Thomas Hutchinson's ear. "The minute that door opens, make a mad dash."

He pressed his palm against Thomas's broad back, and Thomas shook it off. That wasn't hard. At 11, he was several stones heavier than the almost-16 Malcolm.

"You don't need to push me!" Thomas hissed back at him. "I know what to do. You told me a hundred times!"

"What are you two whispering about?" said a voice that was suddenly at Thomas's elbow.

Although the light was still dim in the early morning gray of the Swan Tavern's central hall, Thomas knew it was Caroline Taylor looking up at him. Her round, brown eyes and slice-of-melon grin could light up a cave. And Thomas knew her so well that he didn't have to see to know she had her hands planted on her tiny hips.

"Well?" she said, her voice insistent, as if it were tapping its toe.

1

"I was reminding Thomas," Malcolm said, "to make a dash as soon as the doors are opened or none of us will make it."

"Make it to what?" Caroline said suspiciously.

But before Malcolm could answer, a bell clanged, and the knob on one of the double doors jiggled as the Swan Tavern dining room was unlocked from the other side.

"Go!" Malcolm whispered harshly.

Thomas did—nearly plowing down the wigged man in the doorway.

"What on earth, boy?" the man cried, righting his big powdered wig.

But Thomas didn't stop to answer. His deep-set eyes darted across the room for a large table. After all, there would be seven of them—Papa, Mama, Clayton, Malcolm, Patsy, Caroline, and himself.

With a jolt, Thomas spotted the perfect table and dashed toward it. By now, his dark hair was sticking out in all directions and beads of sweat had already formed on his upper lip. He could hear voices gathering behind him and feet scuffling hurriedly to get to breakfast. But nobody was going to get *their* table.

Out of the corner of his eye, he saw someone quickly waddling in the same direction, and Thomas made his final lunge. As he did, their elbows collided. Something round and flat suddenly took flight.

A tray, laden with cups of tea, flew into the air. It came down in a series of crashes, each one more earsplitting than the one before it. When one cup hit just in front of Thomas—who was still hurtling toward the table—his toe caught the spill. Flailing his arms to get his balance, his momentum thrust him forward as if he were diving into a pile of hay. Both hands skidded across the top of the table he'd been headed for, and he jerked to a stop nose to nose with a tiny salt dish.

The voices behind him spiraled up into a chorus of squeals. One sang out above the rest—and its melody wasn't a happy one.

"Thomas Hutchinson, what do you *mean* by this?" boomed the deep bass.

Thomas would rather have buried his face in the sugar bowl than face his father just then. But John Hutchinson's next words were "Get off that table this instant!"—and Thomas did. You didn't argue with Papa . . . especially when he was using The Tone.

Thomas cringed as he backed gingerly away from the tabletop. *He's sure to be wearing The Look, too,* he thought.

He was right. As he looked up the six feet, three inches that made up broad-shouldered John Hutchinson, Thomas saw his bushy, sand-colored eyebrows knitted into an angry knot over his stormy blue eyes and his mouth pressed into a stern, straight line.

"What are you about here?" Papa asked through his teeth. Anyplace else, his father's voice would have been thundering, but Thomas could feel a crowd gathering in the doorway behind them. A gentleman like John Hutchinson didn't "thunder" in public.

"I was only making sure we had a table," Thomas said, his face bright red.

The bushy eyebrows shot up. "For what? Battle?"

"No," Thomas said, "for breakfast."

There were several titters from the doorway—and one smothered guffaw he was sure came from Malcolm.

Papa stared at him. "What on *earth?*"

"I was told," Thomas stammered quickly, "that when the bell rang for breakfast and the doors were unlocked, there would be a general rush into the dining room, and it would take some doing to get an entire table. . . ."

Thomas's voice trailed off as his father's eyes scanned the room. Thomas's followed. He could feel his face turning a deeper shade of red as he saw what his father saw: a few guests staring curiously at them as they chose their tables from the large selection of empty ones that dotted the room. His gaze found Malcolm still stationed in the doorway, stifling his laughter with his hand. Thomas shot him a threatening look before he turned back to Papa. Of course he wouldn't tell his father that his favorite indentured servant boy had put him up to it. There was nothing Papa hated worse than someone telling tales.

John Hutchinson was shaking his handsome, gold-and-silver-haired head down at Thomas. "I see only my youngest son making a fool of himself," he said.

Thomas thought miserably, *Wait until I get hold of Malcolm Donaldson.*

"I don't know where you got such an idea," Papa went on. "There's been no 'general rush' for anything in Yorktown since the revolution started in '76. The last mad dash anyone made here was to get out of town when the Virginia militia took up residency here." He sniffed. "To protect the colony of Virginia from the British. Fine lot of good they've done the Virginians so far."

Thomas let out a cautious puff of relieved air as Papa's mind wandered off to the progress of the war between the Colonists and England. He stabbed another glare in Malcolm's direction. The Scottish boy was holding back his usual square smile, but his black eyes were snapping merrily.

He's not afraid of me for a minute! Thomas thought.

The wiry Malcolm was clever as well as strong. He could outwit and outfight big, fiery-tempered Thomas in just about any situation.

And he's surely not as clumsy as I am.

The man with the wig who had opened the door was on his hands and knees picking up pieces of broken porcelain. A plump maid in a wilted mob cap was beside him, mopping the floor with a rag and muttering under her breath—something about a "spoiled rich boy in an all-fired hurry."

Thomas gnawed on his lip to keep from yelling, *I was just trying to help!*

"Thomas, I'm sure your intentions were good," his father said. "Though heaven knows where you get these notions." To Thomas's surprise, John Hutchinson gave a soft chuckle. "Mr. Gibbons," he called.

The man on the floor stood up and tugged at the bottom of his brown Holland vest.

"Yes, sir, Mr. Hutchinson?" he said.

"My son was concerned that our party might not find a table for breakfast this morning. Could you direct us to one?"

The little man gave Papa a dignified half-smile and wafted a hand toward the very table Thomas had made his landing on.

"You and your guests will be seated here if it suits you," Mr. Gibbons said. "Even if I were overrun with guests, I would still reserve my best table for a gentleman such as yourself, Mr. Hutchinson." The man's wig seemed to tighten on his head as his voice rose in pitch. "I was, in fact, honored that you decided to lodge with us last night, rather than at your own plantation. I hope you found everything satisfactory upstairs."

He rubbed his hands together and dug his eyes into Papa's face, waiting for the torrent of compliments he was obviously accustomed to. Papa politely gave him a few while Thomas looked back at the little knot of people in the doorway. Malcolm was still shoving down his laughter, and Thomas gave him an *I'll get you* look. Caroline was tucking her blonde hair under her cap and looking from one of them to the other in mild disgust.

She's used to us getting each other into trouble, Thomas decided with relief. *She won't stay mad at me for long.*

He knew he didn't need to worry about Patsy, Malcolm's 10-year-old sister who was planted between them. Though just a year younger than Thomas and Caroline, she looked up to all of them as if they were the Three Wise Men. Right now she was gazing up at her big brother with her huge green eyes and then flipping her dark braids back in Caroline's direction and smiling so that a tiny dimple appeared under each eye. As long as the quiet little waif was included in the doings of the Fearsome Foursome, she didn't seem to much care what they did.

Thomas moved his eyes on. Mama was there, too, looking powdered and poised in her pale-blue gown and her white gauze shawl and matching cap—even in the summer dampness. Her hair—black like Thomas's, though never askew like his— framed her pretty face and her gray eyes, creating the picture of elegance. It didn't seem to matter that a war raged on in the colonies around them or that her son had just flown across a tavern table like an out-of-control water fowl.

And then there was his oldest brother, Clayton. He was not likely to remain unruffled after the scene Thomas had just made. There would probably be an angry red smear on each pale cheek, his gray eyes were most likely raging like a pair of thunderclouds, and the powder from his hair had very possibly been shaken all over the narrow shoulders of his velvet waistcoat as he'd shuddered.

Clayton hates it when I'm not the perfect gentlemen he tried to teach me to be, Thomas thought.

Twenty-year-old Clayton was indeed standing next to Mama, dressed without a wrinkle in a pale lavender traveling suit, with every strand of tawny hair perfectly powdered and combed.

But Thomas had to look twice to be sure it was Clayton. There was no disappointed look on his face. His eyes weren't saying, *You've done it again, Thomas. How could you?*

Clayton didn't look as if he'd even seen Thomas make a scene. His eyes looked vaguely in the direction of the center table, but the mind behind them was obviously far away.

He's probably halfway to England already, Thomas thought. That brought him back with a jolt to the reason they were all in Yorktown this morning in the first place.

He looked guiltily at the maid who was scooping up the last of the shattered china.

I just wanted to hurry things along, he thought. *And I've only slowed them down. What if Clayton misses the ship?*

"Ah, all is ready, Mr. Hutchinson!" Mr. Gibbons said, shooing the maid away with one hand and waving grandly toward the table with the other. "Please be seated, you and your party." He clapped both hands smartly at the maid. "A tray of tea for the Hutchinsons at once!"

"That's what I was a-doin' before that mad cow come a-stormin' in here," she muttered under her breath as she waddled toward the kitchen.

Thomas swallowed and lurched for the table. Papa caught him by the shoulder and held him there until everyone was seated. Thomas glared at Malcolm again as he slunk into the seat between Caroline and Clayton.

Papa cleared his throat. "Normally, I would have Clayton ask the grace," he said. "His being the minister in our family—"

"About to *become* a minister," Clayton put in.

"But since he is embarking on a long journey today, I would like to have the honor of sending him off with a blessing." Papa nodded respectfully toward Clayton. "If I may?"

Clayton nodded back and Papa began praying.

"Father, please grant Clayton a safe journey. Please calm the waters with Your almighty hands, and part the sea of hate that he will walk into in England, so that he may be ordained as one of Your ministers and return safely to lead Your congregation here in America. Amen."

There was a murmur of amens around the table, and heads bobbed up. Mama's gray eyes were misty.

"I wish there were some way you could be ordained right here in Virginia," she said.

"Now, Mama," Clayton said patiently. "You know I need a bishop of the Church of England to ordain me, and we have none here in the colonies."

"We always thought we might get one, before the war," Papa said. "Now there isn't a chance—until we've won our independence and can have bishops of our own."

"And I didn't want to wait that long," Clayton said.

That's for sure, Thomas thought. *I remember all the arguments at the table and behind Papa's library door.*

Clayton had been fighting for permission to go to

England to be ordained ever since he'd finished at the divinity school at the College of William and Mary a year ago, and Papa's answer had always been no—especially with the smallpox raging over there. Clayton could barely survive a cold, much less a dreaded disease.

And then Nicholas came along, Thomas thought. He grinned to himself. Working in the apothecary shop every afternoon for old Francis Pickering, Thomas had at first thought the gangly Dr. Nicholas Quincy was a sissy. But he was the one who had won this battle for Clayton. First he'd found a way to help him through his heart spells and grow stronger so they wouldn't come so often. And then he'd learned about a doctor in Massachusetts who had found a vaccine for smallpox. He'd sent for some and given it to Clayton.

"Ah, here we are!" cried Mr. Gibbons. Two steaming trays were set on the table, and Thomas saw Malcolm's and Patsy's eyes widen. They were used to a bowl of mush and maybe the occasional sugar muffin before they hurried off to work, Malcolm for the Hutchinsons and Patsy for Lydia Clark, the lady she was indentured to. To be invited to sit at the table with the family and share in a celebration was a rare treat for a servant in buckskin breeches like Malcolm or a loose gown made from mattress ticking like Patsy.

It isn't rare in our house, though, Thomas thought proudly. *Papa believes in what the war for independence is about— everybody being equal.*

Mr. Gibbons stood rubbing his hands together as he watched the two black servants unload their trays onto the table. There were plates heaped with fish, clams, oysters, crab, and shrimp, and others piled high with chicken and ham. The servants freckled the table with big bowls of berries, nuts, and fruits, and even bigger dishes of corn pone, hoe cake, and batter bread.

Papa sighed as he stirred his tea. "My only regret about this war is that we can't get real tea anymore," he said.

"Your *only* regret, Father?" Clayton said. His thin lips twitched into a smile. "If I recall correctly, at first you didn't even want a war!"

"I didn't," Papa said. "I thought we would settle our differences with England and procure our independence peacefully." He shook his big head sadly. "It seems I was wrong. Lives are being lost every day for the cause."

It was as if a shadow had suddenly passed over the sunny table. Spoons stopped clattering against chargers and porringers, and faces drooped.

Thomas knew what they were thinking. Sam, the second of the three Hutchinson boys, was off who-knew-where in the thick of the fighting. Papa had forbidden him to go, but he'd slipped off to fight for the freedom he so fiercely believed in. Thomas missed him so much that it hurt to think about him.

Thomas's eyes flickered at Caroline next to him. She was staring down at her porringer without a trace of the slice-of-melon smile.

She's thinking about Alexander, Thomas thought, with another stab in his chest that always came when he thought about Caroline's brother. He had been Thomas's tutor—and friend—before he had disappeared the same night Sam had gone off to join the army. Only in Alexander's case, *which* side he'd gone off to join was still anybody's guess.

He told Sam he was pretending to be on the side of the British, Thomas remembered. *Anybody would believe that, since Caroline and Alexander's father is still loyal to the king.* But Alexander had also told Sam he was really a spy for the Patriots. Unlike his Loyalist father, he said he believed America should be its own free country.

Thomas looked at Caroline's sad face again. *But he told his father he really was going to fight with the British.*

Thomas's mouth went dry, and he put his fork back in his porringer with a piece of ham still stuck on its prongs. If Alexander were a Patriot spy and was captured by the British, he'd be hanged for sure. And if he were fighting for the British and the Patriots of Virginia got hold of him, his future wasn't worth much more. And neither was Papa's. He had vouched for the Loyalist Taylors, promising they'd never take arms against the American cause.

"I owe everyone an apology," Papa said suddenly. "This is a celebration for Clayton. And I have allowed a cloud to pass over it with my talk of the war. Come!" He tapped his spoon gently against his tea cup. "Let us send our Clayton off in joy, eh?"

It was hard for everyone to force their lips to form smiles again, but with Papa calling out toasts for Clayton and Mama laughing her bell laugh and Malcolm saying "Hear! Hear!" through his square grin, it slowly happened.

"A fine meal," Papa said. His deep-blue eyes twinkled. "But can it compare to Esther's cooking?"

Malcolm groaned, and everyone laughed. Esther was the long-time Hutchinson family servant who with her grizzled old husband Otis ran the Williamsburg house where Thomas and his parents now lived. She and Otis loved Malcolm as if he were their own son, but even he could barely stomach her cooking.

"How is everything?" Mr. Gibbons asked as he bustled

over to the table, wringing his hands like a dishrag.

"Everything is wonderful, Lawrence Gibbons," Papa said. "You run as fine an establishment here as Thomas Nelson did when he owned it."

Lawrence Gibbons bowed as if George Washington himself were at the table, and Thomas heard Caroline snort softly.

"Thomas Nelson is now a general in the Virginia militia," Mr. Gibbons said. "I could never hope to live up to that." But he looked eagerly around the table as if he knew someone were going to tell him he was wrong.

"Don't be silly," Mama said. "A well-cooked meal is every bit as important as a well-fought battle."

"That's truer than you know, my dear," Papa said. "Without well-cooked meals our men cannot fight at all—and I fear they aren't getting many."

"I'm afraid you're right," Mr. Gibbons said. "Our last word from the post rider was that Washington's men in New York are still without supplies."

"Well," Papa said, "I have faith that with Nathaniel Greene now in command of our men in Carolina, and Lafayette here in Virginia leading Cornwallis on a merry chase, the tide is about to turn."

Mr. Gibbons grunted. "But you've heard what Benedict Arnold and the British have been doing not far from here—stealing from plantation owners." He cocked his wig curiously. "Is that why you all stayed here last night instead of out on the Hutchinson Homestead? To avoid an attack by that miserable traitor?"

"No," Papa said firmly. "We stayed here because I had business at the courthouse across the street late yesterday and because we wanted an early start for the harbor to put my son aboard the *Mary Jones*."

That was exactly the explanation Papa had given,
Thomas remembered, when he had begged Papa to let them
go to the plantation first. Before he'd been sent to
Williamsburg more than a year ago, the Hutchinson
Homestead was the only home Thomas had ever known,
and he loved it. To be this close, just a few miles away, was
like seeing a jar of cinnamon drops on Francis's counter and
not being able to taste even one.

But of course, there had been no arguing with Papa.

"We must be about our business now," John Hutchinson
said as he stood, his chair scraping against the wood floor.

"Of course, sir, and I wish you a safe journey!" Mr.
Gibbons bounced his wig in Clayton's direction.

Suddenly, the dining room door was flung open and a
sweaty man stood in the doorway, threw back his head, and
sent out a loud, endless blare on the horn he pressed to his
lips. Caroline plastered her hands over her ears.

"It's the post rider," Thomas shouted over it.

"Really?" Malcolm said mildly. "Who else would come in
here blasting away into everyone's breakfast?"

The post rider pulled the horn away from his mouth and
began to dig into his bag for Mr. Gibbons's mail.

"Well, sir," Papa barked at him. "You've given us all
indigestion, so you might as well tell us what news you have."

"Since you've asked so kindly," the post rider growled at
Papa, "Benedict Arnold and his bloody band have ransacked
the Digges Plantation out on the James River, taken all
their food supplies, and stolen 10 of their male slaves to serve
in the British Army."

Thomas looked quickly at the rest of the Fearsome

Foursome. They looked back with the same surprise he felt.

"Digges!" Caroline whispered to him. "Aren't they the ones who have that wretched Zachary?"

Thomas nodded. The Foursome had given Zachary and his friends a run for their money last spring when they'd tried to bully Thomas at school.

I bet their bullying was nothing compared to Benedict Arnold's, Thomas thought.

"Where is Arnold now?" Papa said to the post rider.

The man gave his brow a swipe and drew himself up proudly. "They say the lousy traitor is going to Portsmouth. He's headed back this way—and he says he won't stop until he's hit every plantation on the York River. *Every* one."

Chapter Two

There was a stunned silence in the Swan Tavern. Clayton cleared his throat.

"Father, shouldn't you get to the homestead right away? I can see myself to the ship."

"No," Papa said. "We will see you off just as we planned. There are times when we cannot be two places at once, and we must turn one place over to God."

But not even Papa could hoist them back up to their former high spirits. It was a glum group that made its way down Ballard Street toward the harbor. Even Caroline, who had never seen Hutchinson Homestead, looked troubled.

"Even though Alexander is fighting for the British," she said to Thomas, "you know he would never do such a thing, don't you?"

Thomas nodded.

She skipped to keep up with his angry strides. "I hope those awful men don't find your plantation," she said.

Thomas shot her a fierce look. "They won't—or they'll

15

have my father to answer to!" he said.

On his other side, Malcolm hitched Patsy up farther on his back where he always carried her. He gave a short laugh and said, "I hate to be sayin' this, lad, but even the great John Hutchinson is no match for an entire company of the British."

"Then what will happen?" Caroline asked.

"Nothing!" Thomas said.

They continued their walk to the harbor in silence. Thomas knew Papa was probably praying. Thomas tried to start his own talk with God.

God? he said in his head. *Please help me to—*

But he stopped. *Help me what?* he thought. *Malcolm is right—even Papa can't stop Benedict Arnold. So what good could I possibly be? I'll probably never see the plantation again.*

That thought made him so sad that he decided not to think about it at all. He focused his eyes on the ship's mast.

The harbor where Clayton's ship was anchored was in the York River. Although it was the shortest, it had the deepest natural channel of the main rivers that led into the Chesapeake Bay. Thomas counted them on his mental fingers, the way Alexander had taught him: the Potomac, the Rappanhanak, the York, and the James. They spread like fingers into the towns on the bay that made up what was called Tidewater, Virginia—Alexandria, Fredericksburg, Richmond, Norfolk, and Yorktown.

Alexander would be proud of me for remembering that, Thomas thought.

As they neared the dock, Thomas could smell the salty, brackish river water. It was a smell that had always gotten his heart racing when he was a little boy and his father had brought him down to the ships he had built as part of his plantation and shipping business. He'd always loved to hear the stories his father would sometimes tell about Thomas's great-grandfather Josiah Hutchinson, who had loved ships and the sea.

But today the smell of the York River and the fish piled on the fishermen's boats made him feel a little sick. It was the way he'd felt when he'd first moved from the plantation to Williamsburg—always longing for what was familiar and safe in the middle of everything that was so new and strange. It smelled like homesickness.

They had reached the dock by now, and Malcolm called out, "There's your trunk, Master Clayton. They're loadin' it aboard right now."

Clayton nodded at the Hutchinson trunk with its brass latches and hinges that Otis had lovingly polished for him and Esther had folded freshly laundered shirts into and Papa had dropped off at his shipping office last night.

"This is good-bye, Mother," Clayton said—a little stiffly, Thomas thought.

But that was Clayton. He was much different from good-natured Sam and fiery Thomas.

Clayton faced his father and put out his hand. Papa gripped it with both of his as if he didn't want to let go. Thomas found himself swallowing hard.

Papa finally pulled his hands away, and Clayton turned to Thomas. He put out his hand, and for a moment, Thomas only looked at it. He wanted to hurl himself at Clayton and hug him and say, "Don't go! You're too sickly. You'll never come back!"

Thomas put his pawlike hand into Clayton's frail one. "Godspeed," Thomas said, the way he'd heard Papa say it to friends who'd gone off on long journeys.

"Remember, Thomas—" Clayton started to say. And then he bit back the words and said instead, "You've become a fine young man. I'm proud to call you brother." He pulled his hand away. "God be with you," he said, and he went up the gangplank with his halting walk and disappeared aboard the ship as if he'd been swallowed by it. A sick wave washed over Thomas.

Something clutched his arm, and Thomas looked down to see his mother's tiny hand clawing at his sleeve. Her face was working like a butter churn, tears shimmering in her eyes.

Papa turned from the end of the dock and came toward them. His face was calm. Mama grabbed at his hand.

"Not to worry, my dear," Papa said, squeezing her hand. "This is of God. He will bridge the gap between what Clayton needs and what we can give him. He always does when we're doing His work."

Thomas watched as the sailors pulled up the gangplank, leaving several yards of river between them and Clayton. The sails flapped crisply on the summer breeze of the bay, and the *Mary Jones* began to move away.

We would need *a bridge to get to him now,* Thomas thought. *Please be the bridge, God,* he prayed.

Caroline, Malcolm, and Patsy had hung back until the big ship was under way and moving out of the harbor. When Thomas couldn't watch it anymore and turned toward the street, Caroline ran to him and tugged on his shirtsleeve.

"I just thought of something, Tom," she said.

"What?"

"Now that Clayton's actually gone, he's that much closer to coming home!"

"I like that, Mistress Taylor," Papa said. "We need your cheerful mind around us right now." Then he turned to Patsy. "And we need your smile." She beamed up at him, smiling her charming, crooked-toothed smile. "And I have an idea how we can do that," he said.

Mama dabbed at her eyes with a handkerchief. "Let's hear it, John. I could use a happy idea."

Papa motioned the group into a circle. A gull squawked mournfully overhead, mocking the sad way Thomas felt. He wasn't sure he wanted to be cheered up.

"I've given it some thought since we spoke to the post rider," Papa said. "If Benedict Arnold has just left the Digges plantation all the way up the James on the other side of Williamsburg, he won't reach our homestead for days, if indeed he ever does. It's safe there now, and I'm of a mind to check in on the place and see what I can do to batten it down in case of attack. Clayton hired an overseer to look after the place in his absence, and it will do no harm for me to check on him as well. I say we go to the plantation, all of us, and enjoy its peace for a short time. I can send a messenger to your father, Caroline, and your mistress, Patsy. I'm certain they can spare you for another day or two."

Thomas stared at his father. They were going to the plantation? And taking Malcolm, Patsy, and Caroline with them?

"What's the matter, Thomas?" Papa asked. "Don't you like the idea?"

"Yes, sir!" Thomas cried. He backed up the street at a trot so he could still see his father as he went. "May we go now—right now?"

"Not if you run into that water trough and fall into it," Papa said. "Then you'll be a disgrace to the family, and we'll have to pack you off to Williamsburg."

Thomas whirled and narrowly avoided tumbling bottom first into a horse trough. Malcolm threw his shaggy black head back and howled.

"See him and the young ladies to the carriage, Malcolm," Papa said, chuckling. "I'm right behind you."

Malcolm grabbed for his arm, but Thomas dodged him and took off at a run for the Hutchinsons' carriage, which was waiting at the tavern. He could hear Caroline shrieking as she ran to catch up, and he knew Malcolm would be beside him as soon as he scooped Patsy up onto his back.

"I'm actually going to the homestead, Tom!" Caroline said happily. "You've told me so much about it that I feel like I've already been there. Let's see, there's the staircase as big as my whole *house* in Williamsburg and the fields that stretch on longer than the Duke of Gloucester Street—"

Thomas ducked his head. "Well, I might have exaggerated a little."

"Oh, I know, Tom," she said, grinning. "But if it's even half as grand as you say, I can't wait!"

It was, Thomas knew, and he couldn't wait either as he scrambled up into the driver's seat to wait for Malcolm, who folded the steps down for the girls and helped them up. The carriage rocked as they, and then Mama and Papa, climbed in for the several-mile drive.

"Burgess and Judge can pull faster than you think," Thomas said as Malcolm joined him and picked up the reins.

Malcolm grinned his square smile. "I'll get us there soon enough, lad," he said. "Don't you worry."

But it couldn't *be* soon enough for Thomas as he perched on the edge of his seat. Everything he'd missed for more than a year was suddenly all around him.

Tobacco Road Valley with its groves of bamboo growing side by side with the red and white mulberry trees and the silvery-trunked crepe myrtles . . . the gently rolling hills hugged by the hands of the tidal waters . . . the forest floors alive with yellow-flowered adder's tongue and trout lilies. And everywhere the birds—warblers and thrushes and scarlet tanagers, orioles and flycatchers and indigo buntings. Thomas leaned out so far to get a glimpse of his favorite—the redwing blackbird that sang in the marshes—that Malcolm had to grab his arm and keep him from falling off the carriage.

"Whoa there, lad!"

"I can't help it. It's beautiful. Isn't it the most beautiful place you've ever seen?"

Malcolm had to nod. "That it is, lad. That it is."

It seemed to Thomas that it took half a lifetime to get to the long road that led straight up to Hutchinson Homestead. Finally, before he could see the two rows of oak trees that lined the drive, he smelled it—the river, the honeysuckles, and the newly cut wheat.

"There it is, Malcolm!" he cried, standing up on the seat.

Malcolm let the reins go slack, and his lower lip, too. Thomas looked down to see him staring at the sight before him with his black eyes popping.

"That's your house, lad?" he said finally.

"That's it," Thomas said proudly.

He gazed at the stately brick mansion with its two wings and six chimneys, and he knew he felt just as much wonder seeing it for the hundredth time as Malcolm must have on his first. With all its shiny windows and green shutters, and its wide welcoming front door and its perfect carpet of green lawn that stretched on forever—it was a wondrous house. It was *his* house.

He could hear Caroline squealing from inside the carriage, and he stretched down to peer into the side window.

"May Caroline and Patsy get out here and run up the road with me?" he asked.

Mama laughed her tinkle of a laugh, and Papa said, "Yes, and you might as well take Malcolm, too. I'll drive the carriage the rest of the way."

The four of them were tearing up the road toward the house before Papa could even pick up the reins. Thomas led the way, breathing in the home air and shouting all the way.

"Look there—out on the water—it's a blue heron! See the apple orchard? We make cider every fall! Over there, Malcolm—there's the stable! You've never seen so many stalls. Oh, and Caroline, you can climb every tree in those woods if you want! We won't see you for days!"

He didn't stop calling out landmarks until they reached the front steps. Then all Thomas could do was stand and look around. It was even more magnificent than he remembered.

Papa pulled the carriage to a dusty stop at the bottom of the front steps and hopped to the ground to help Mama out.

The front door came open and a small-faced woman poked her head out. She wore a maid's cap and apron and a surprised look. Her eyes glossed over Thomas and headed for the steps.

"Master Hutchinson!" she said. "I wasn't expecting you today!"

"It's all right, Mattie," Papa said. "We had a change of plans."

"Hello, Mattie!" Mama called out. "Are there enough rooms ready for all these people?"

"I'll be sleeping in the servants' quarters," Malcolm said at once. "My sister and I."

"You do as you choose, Malcolm," Papa said as he led Mama up the steps. "But Patsy is here as our guest. Perhaps she'd like to share a room with Caroline."

Thomas thought Patsy's green eyes would burst from her face. She smiled and then turned red and then hid behind Malcolm.

"I think that settles it, then," Mama said, laughing. "A room for Caroline and Patsy together. Thomas can stay in his old room, of course."

Mattie looked around blankly. "Thomas, ma'am?"

"Right beside you," Papa said.

Mattie looked at Thomas and took a step backward.

"This is Master Thomas?" she said.

"He's grown, hasn't he?" Mama said.

Mattie continued to stare as Papa pulled the front door wide open.

"Ladies and gentlemen," he said, "welcome to my home."

Thomas started to plunge in first, and then remembered to let the girls go. Mattie stared at him harder than ever, but she couldn't match the looks on Caroline's and Patsy's faces as they gasped at the entrance hall.

Thomas had always been so busy shinnying up trees and chasing sheep that he'd never taken time to notice how beautiful the Hutchinson Homestead mansion was on the inside. He tried to imagine what his three friends must have been thinking as they gazed around.

Have you ever seen such rugs? They must have come straight from the Orient.

Oh, my. What a magnificent staircase! A prince could ride a horse up that!

Does someone polish that case clock every day? And that gold-framed looking glass? And the porcelain lamp stands?

Malcolm was the first to speak. "Who is that in the portrait, sir, if I may ask?"

He was pointing to a painting on the wall at the bottom of the staircase.

"That is my father, Daniel Hutchinson," Papa answered. "Thomas's grandfather."

"He looks like a noble man, sir," Malcolm said.

Thomas examined the painting. He must have passed it at least a thousand times in his life as he'd flown down the staircase or, at Sam's urging, slid down the banister. But he wasn't sure he'd ever stopped to really look at it before.

He wasn't sure now, seeing the tight expression on Grandfather Daniel's square face, that he was exactly noble. Stern, maybe. And definitely in charge. He looked a little like Clayton. Thomas felt another wave of sickness.

"And who are these?" Caroline asked. She pointed to a portrait on the other side of the hall, by the entrance to the drawing room.

"Oh, now we go further back in time," Papa said. He put a hand gently near the tall, square-shouldered man in the painting who was flanked on one side by a dark-haired woman and on the other by a younger version of her, about 17 years old. Behind them stood a young man Malcolm's age with thick blond curls and deep-set blue eyes.

"This is my great-grandfather, Joseph Hutchinson," Papa

said of the man in the middle. "He brought his family to Virginia in 1692 from Salem Village, Massachusetts, to escape the crumbling of the church there at that time." Papa smiled at the painting as if Joseph Hutchinson could see him. "He was a man ahead of his time. He was a Puritan, and the Puritans didn't believe in such frivolous things as having portraits painted. But after a few years here, building his plantation, Joseph decided it was important to have his image passed down to his descendants." Papa laughed softly. "I understand he threw off many of the stifling restrictions of the Puritan church. No one told Joseph Hutchinson how to live his life except God Himself."

"Who are the others?" Caroline asked.

"That lovely woman there is his wife, Deborah," Mama said. "And that is their daughter, Hope. I've read Hope's diaries. They tell quite a story of their life in Massachusetts and here. She was almost as much a rebel as her father."

"What about the boy?" Malcolm asked.

Thomas looked curiously at the group now gathered in front of the portrait. He'd never seen people take such interest in his old relatives.

"That would be Josiah Hutchinson," Papa said. "My grandfather, and Thomas's great-grandfather. He was the one who built up the Hutchinson shipyard. He loved the sea as if it were his son—though fortunately he took the time to have a real son or Thomas and I wouldn't be here. Josiah was quite a man, very close to his God. He joined the Church of England and was quite a force in building up the church here in Yorktown and ridding it of many of the old English formal traditions."

"Josiah looks like you, Tom!" Caroline said.

Thomas stared at the painting and shook his head. "He has blond hair. I have black."

"It's the eyes," she said.

"By heaven, I think you're right," Papa said. He stepped closer to the painting and squinted at it. "Dark blue. Set deep in his face."

"They're like yours, too, sir," said a soft voice.

Patsy was peeking out from behind Malcolm, looking shyly up at John Hutchinson. They all stared. It was rare for Patsy to talk at all—and rarer still for her to speak up to someone like this big man.

Papa looked from her to the painting to Thomas and then back again.

"Indeed, we all have it!" Papa said. "Old Joseph, too!"

"You come from a long line of clear-seeing men, sir," Malcolm said.

Papa studied the painting for a moment before he looked back at Malcolm. "It's a gift from God, then," he said.

It seemed to be most of forever, Thomas thought, before he had a chance to show the rest of the plantation to Malcolm, Caroline, and Patsy. There were the bags to take upstairs and play clothes to be borrowed from the servants' children and lunch to be eaten in the parlor, served with maddening slowness by Mattie and two little servant girls who had shot up like weeds since Thomas had sat in the schoolroom upstairs with them two years ago. They looked warily at Thomas as they served the chicken-and-dumpling soup.

"Why were those girls afraid of you, Tom?" Caroline asked when they were finally allowed to dash out the back door to explore.

"Afraid of me?"

"They were quakin' in their slippers," Malcolm said.

Thomas shrugged. "I don't know. I guess it's because I'm tall now."

Malcolm just snorted.

"Come on," Thomas said. "I'll show you all the best places to play."

It was a wonderful afternoon for the Fearsome Foursome.

They chased each other through the maze of gardens that stretched all the way from the back door to the river. They hid from each other in the wheat and cornfields and made each other squeal with surprise attacks. When it got too hot to run any more, they gathered in the stable and tumbled into the hay to talk and chew on straws. Malcolm looked around admiringly at the rows of leather bridles and harnesses hanging on hooks on the walls.

"I thought the stable in Williamsburg was somethin'," he said. "But this . . . this beats all." He fingered a leather strap that lay split open on the table. "I feel like I should be workin'."

"Papa says you came on the trip as our guest, and you're to be treated like one," Thomas said.

"I love your papa."

Patsy was lying in the hay beside Caroline, staring dreamily at the ceiling. Caroline came up on one elbow and grinned down at her.

"You do, Patsy? You love Master John Hutchinson?"

"He said I was a young lady."

"Well, you are, then!" said Caroline.

"Patsy."

Her name was spoken so sharply by Malcolm that

Thomas caught his breath. Malcolm never used anything but the kindest tone with his little sister.

Patsy seemed to shrink into the hay. "What?"

"Don't be fancyin' yourself a proper lady just because some rich gentleman says you are." He glanced at Thomas. "Beggin' your pardon, lad. Your papa's a fine man and he's done right by me, but this war we're fightin' is about everyone bein' equal because they are who they are and they earn it—not because someone who's born to it gives them the right."

"Is that why you wanted to sleep in the servants' hall in the kitchen building?" Thomas asked.

Malcolm nodded firmly. "I don't need favors. I know who I am."

Caroline sat up straight in the hay and flung her arm around Patsy's shoulders. "That's fine, Malcolm Donaldson," she said, her brown eyes glaring at him, "but you had no business scolding Patsy like that. Look at her. You've made her cry!"

Malcolm rolled his eyes and scrunched his mouth up at one corner. "Don't be cryin', lassie," he said to his sister. "Come on. I didn't mean to hurt your—"

"Well, you did!" Caroline said. She put both arms around Patsy and scowled at Malcolm. "You could be more careful."

Malcolm looked helplessly at Thomas, who shrugged. He'd never claimed to understand girls at all, even Caroline. He only knew the whole scene was making him squirm. He nodded toward the door, and Malcolm followed him gratefully out into the sun.

"Caroline's turnin' her into a sissy," Malcolm muttered.

"Want to see the rest of the horses?" Thomas asked.

They were halfway to the fenced area where the Hutchinsons' other dozen horses were grazing lazily after a day's work in the fields when Caroline and Patsy caught up to them. Caroline dropped Patsy's hand and stood on the bottom rung of the fence. Thomas climbed up beside her.

"They're beautiful!" she cried. "Look how their tails hang all the way to the ground!"

"What is that one's name?" Patsy asked.

Thomas looked a little sadly at the gray, dappled horse she was pointing at. "That was Sam's horse. He called him Patriot."

Caroline stretched out a hand to beckon to him. "Can we feed them an apple or something?"

"You give those animals one bit of anything, and I'll have your hides—all of you!" said a voice from the path.

They all whirled around, and Thomas nearly fell off the fence.

Behind them stood the biggest man he'd ever seen, and he was pushing his sleeves up past his elbows with angry hands.

"Now get away from those horses!" he shouted. "Go on, all of you!"

✛-✚-✛

Chapter Three

No one, not even Mr. We're-All-Equal-Here Malcolm, argued with the man. He was half again the size of Papa with none of John Hutchinson's well-bred gentleness. His hands were clenched at his sides, as hard and crusty-looking as tree bark, and his mud-colored eyes were ringed in angry red.

"I said get away from those horses!" he shouted again. "Where are you supposed to be, anyway? Get back to your jobs, ya plebeian herd!"

If he had *had* a job, Thomas would surely have gone back to it immediately. The man's mouth was tightened into a mean line, and Thomas didn't want to wait around to hear what would come out of it next. He leaped from the fence and tore back toward the stables, and he could hear the rest of the "herd" following him. He could also feel the red-rimmed eyes watching them as they ran.

"What's a plebeian herd?" Caroline whispered as she scurried along beside him.

"It means a bunch of common slaves!" Malcolm hissed from Thomas's other side. "He thinks we're all your father's servants, lad!"

Thomas stopped and looked back over his shoulder. Red Eyes was still staring them down. "Why?"

"Because we're all dressed that way," Malcolm said. "You ought to go back and set him straight—at least for yourself and Caroline."

"No, Tom!" Caroline tugged at Thomas's arm. "Let him think what he wants. That man is *evil!* I can see it in his eyes!"

But once again the gigantic man bellowed.

"Do I have to come after you with a whip? Get back to work!"

The Fearsome Foursome fled like a quartet of startled geese back toward the stable.

"You've no business there either!" Red Eyes hollered.

"Follow me!" Thomas hissed, and then he took off behind the stable and into a stand of trees several yards from it. All he could hear behind him were three sets of pounding feet and the crashing of branches—and a monstrous voice shouting, "Come back here! Come back or I'll put the whip to ya!"

Thomas didn't stop until he'd reached a marshy area near the river—and the shouting had faded.

Thomas collapsed against a tree, and Caroline crumpled in a heap at his feet. Malcolm crashed in beside them with Patsy on his back.

"Is he coming?" Caroline asked.

Malcolm shook his head, wiping sweat from his brow. "A big cow like that can run only so far."

"Who *is* that horrible man, Tom?" Caroline demanded. With Red Eyes half a mile away, her bravery was returning.

"I don't know! I never saw him before!"

"He obviously never saw you before either," Malcolm said. "Like I was sayin', he mistook you both for servants."

Caroline frowned. "Does your father treat all his servants that way?"

"No!" Thomas cried.

Malcolm shook his head. "I *am* one of his servants, and he's never called me one of the plebeian herd."

Patsy was shaking her head, too, and frowning fiercely at Caroline.

Caroline laughed. "I only wanted to feed the horses."

By now Malcolm had caught his breath, and his black eyes were raging. "Whoever he is, I'd like to be givin' him a piece of my mind, I would!"

Thomas settled himself on a stump and plucked a piece of sweet grass to chew on. "I guess he's used to saying whatever he wants—a man that big. He looks like he could tear out one of these oak trees and swing it at you!"

Caroline shook out her blonde hair from under the servant's cap she'd been wearing and twisted her mouth. "You're big, Thomas, and you don't go around threatening people with whips. And neither does your papa."

"Size helps," Malcolm said. "But it's meanness that does it. I saw some cruel men when I was stealin' on the streets with my father in Scotland. You can see it in their eyes. I would like to tell him a thing or two!"

"Do it, Malcolm!" Caroline said. "I'd like to see you do it!"

While Malcolm proceeded to demonstrate how he would cut Red Eyes down to size, Thomas slid down in front of the stump and gnawed at the inside of his mouth.

That big, ugly man must work for Papa now, he told himself. *He wouldn't be thinking he could give anybody orders here if he didn't. But why would Papa hire someone so . . . so mean?*

And Malcolm was right. It was more the meanness than the size of him that had sent Thomas's heart right up into his throat. Thomas hadn't even thought to say, "I'm John Hutchinson's son!" He'd never had anyone treat him as if he were a snake that had to be driven out of the garden. All he'd wanted to do was get away.

"So are you going to tell your papa?" Caroline said.

"I don't know," Thomas said. "It sounds like tattling."

"Do you want my advice, lad?" Malcolm said.

Thomas shrugged.

"I say don't tell your father anything yet. Let's show this big gorilla that we're not to be yelled at, eh?"

"As long as he doesn't break out his whip before we show him!" Caroline said.

Patsy whimpered and scooted next to Malcolm.

Thomas gnawed his lip some more. *I don't like him being here. But if I run to Papa, I'm still the brat everyone around here remembers.*

"All right," he said finally. "We can take care of Red Eyes ourselves."

"That's right," Malcolm said. He grabbed Patsy and pulled her belly-first onto his feet and stuck them into the air. She squealed as he twirled her around. "We're the Fearsome Foursome, right? We can do anything!"

Thomas smiled and nodded. But when he looked at Caroline, he knew she wasn't so sure.

And deep inside, he wasn't either.

Unlike in Williamsburg, where there was a big dinner at

noon and a light supper in the evening, two big, hot meals were served at the plantation every day, and that night's supper was held in the elegant dining room, behind the drawing room on the main floor of the mansion. Thomas could see from the stairs, as he came down in one of Sam's old suits that had been left in his clothes press, that the table was set with his great-grandmother's china and silverware and Mama's snowy white linen tablecloth and napkins. There were two silver candelabra fitted with green candles and several quintal vases of red roses from Mattie's garden.

Patsy's going to think she's died and gone to heaven, Thomas thought.

He was more interested in the food. He'd grown up on Cookie's baked shad, potato balls, and watermelon pickles. Suffering Esther's cooking for the last year had been like being on prison rations. He drooled just thinking about what lay in store on that table.

Caroline scooted down the stairs behind him and jumped from the bottom step so she could twirl in front of him. She was wearing a filmy pink dress with more ribbons than he had ever seen in the milliner's shop on any one day.

"Where did you get that?" he asked.

"Your mama," she said. "She got it out of a trunk upstairs. It belonged to your papa's sister when she lived here as a little girl. Wait till you see Patsy. Your mama has her *all* done up." Caroline grinned slyly. "She says it's nice to have *girls* to dress for a change."

Thomas was about to yank at one of her ribbons when something caught his eye from the top of the stairs, and he looked up instead.

Mama was there looking more like a queen than Thomas

had seen her since they'd gone to Williamsburg. She had been too busy lately, making bandages for the soldiers and praying with the other ladies over the war, to dress like that anymore.

But it was the little person at her side that riveted Thomas's gaze. It was Patsy, all in white that looked brilliant against her black hair, now in bouncy curls instead of two thick braids. She wore even more ribbons than Caroline, and there was barely an inch of her that wasn't trimmed with lace. She had obviously just peeked at herself in the looking glass, because she looked as stunned as Thomas felt.

"That was your Aunt Elizabeth's dress, too," Caroline said. "Doesn't it look as if it were made for her?"

Thomas didn't know about that. He just knew she didn't look like Patsy anymore. She could have been a princess, wafting down the stairs holding Mama's hand.

"She'll be moonin' over that for months now," a voice muttered behind them.

"Don't you spoil this for her, Malcolm Donaldson!" Caroline said between her teeth, her slice-of-melon smile still perfectly intact. "Or you'll have me to answer to!"

Malcolm nodded in disgust and headed for the dining room. He, too, was in one of Sam's left-behind suits, and he looked uncomfortable in its silk taffeta. Thomas would have teased him—if he hadn't felt just as ridiculous in the violet-colored silk suit Mama had laid out for him.

Caroline swept into the dining room. As soon as her back was turned, Malcolm deposited a frown on Patsy. But even that couldn't darken the evening for her—not when Papa stood up from the table when she entered the room and said, "My, my, I've never seen so much beauty and elegance in one room."

Malcolm groaned under his breath and went to his chair. Patsy floated to hers.

Thomas was sure he'd never tasted a better meal. There was jellied soup, new peas, and corn fritters—and baked shad and potato balls just the way he remembered them, perhaps better. Mattie kept piling the silver baskets with hot bread, and Thomas kept spreading slices with preserves, three different kinds at once. There was barely room for the brown sugar cakes with pecans that were served for dessert, but he managed to squeeze in a few. As he popped the last cake into his mouth, there was a tap at the dining room door.

"That would be Dawson Chorley," Papa said to Mama as Mattie bustled to open it. "He's the one Clayton hired to oversee the plantation in his absence. I asked him to join us for dessert and coffee so we can begin to discuss a few matters. I hope you don't mind, my dear."

"Not at all," Mama said graciously.

Thomas shot Caroline and Malcolm a look across the table that said, *I'll try to get us excused as fast as I can. This will be plenty boring!*

But both Caroline and Malcolm froze as they looked at the figure who darkened the dining room doorway, and Thomas froze with them. Patsy did everything but crawl under her chair.

The man at the door was Red Eyes.

"Mr. Chorley!" Papa said, standing up and extending a hospitable hand.

"Mr. Hutchinson, sir!" Red Eyes replied as he crossed the room. "How kind of you to invite me in. I hope I'm not intruding on your family gathering."

"Nonsense!" John Hutchinson said as he gripped Red Eyes' hands warmly and shook them. He nodded toward

Mama. "My wife, Virginia Hutchinson."

Mama smiled, and Red Eyes went to her and kissed her hand as if he were George Washington himself. Thomas blinked four times and stared. This couldn't be the same man who had chased them halfway through the woods this afternoon.

"My youngest son, Thomas," Papa was saying. He motioned to Thomas, who cringed in his seat. *The minute this man sees me,* he thought frantically, *all this politeness is going to go right out that window.*

But Red Eyes—Dawson Chorley, Papa had called him— put out his hand to shake Thomas's and smiled into his eyes. Those were the same red-ringed eyes all right. But this man nodded respectfully to Thomas and did the same to Patsy, Malcolm, and Caroline as they were introduced as the Hutchinsons' guests. It was obvious he didn't think he'd ever seen any of them before in his life.

Dawson was seated at the table to Papa's left and was deep into conversation with him before Thomas dared look at Caroline or the Donaldsons. They all looked as if a three-headed elephant had just charged through the room. And Malcolm looked as if he wanted to spear it.

"I think you children may be excused," Mama said in a low voice. "Mattie will serve a light snack before bed if you haven't had enough to eat."

But food was the farthest thing from their minds as they tried to exit the dining room in a dignified fashion—and then bolted for the sitting room on the wing beyond the library. Thomas couldn't get the door closed fast enough before Malcolm popped open like a cider jug.

"He's the new overseer!"

"He's going to take Clayton's place?" Caroline said. "I

feel sorry for Mattie and the rest of the servants! He'll be whipping them for sure."

"But he seemed like a gentleman in there," Patsy said, fingering one of her white ribbons.

"You've had your head turned with all this lady-and-gentleman treatment!" Malcolm scowled. "But he did act the part, didn't he?"

"He didn't even seem like the same person!" Caroline said. She nudged Thomas. "Do you think so, Tom?"

Thomas looked up from playing with the silver button on his cuff and shook his head. "He acted like he never saw us before."

"He didn't!" Malcolm said. His eyes were flashing, and he barely stopped himself from smashing his fist on the walnut game table. "What he saw out there today were four *servant* children trying to get out of work. What he saw in the dining room just now were four *rich* children being properly served their watermelon pickles!"

Caroline looked down at her pink-ribboned dress. "I suppose we do look different."

"It shouldn't matter," Malcolm said.

"You wanted us to show him that we weren't to be yelled at," Patsy said timidly.

"Not with fancy clothes and servants all around us!" Malcolm said. His voice seemed to cut through her, and she sank back into the plush velvet chair she was sitting in.

Caroline shot him a dark look.

"How did you want us to show him?" Thomas asked.

"By who we are," Malcolm said.

"Who are we?" Caroline asked.

"Equal to him, that's sure!" Malcolm said.

His eyes had a glint Thomas had seen there before—when Malcolm was on a mission he wouldn't be stopped from going on. Thomas chewed hard on the inside of his mouth. Malcolm seldom went on one of his missions alone.

"It's not so hard for you and Thomas," Malcolm was saying to Caroline. "You've never had to fight for your place in the world. But Patsy and I, we have. That's why I want so badly to win this war with England—so we can have the chance to live any way we want." He balled up his wiry fists. "I don't want it given to me, mind you. I'm willin' to work for it, and I will. But if we're all equal—the way we will be when we're free—we'll have respect given us along the way. Don't you see?"

Thomas did see. But that didn't help with the thoughts that were chasing each other around in *his* mind, the ones about Dawson Chorley. It was as if this man had two faces . . . and *he* was going to be running their plantation. His beloved homestead.

"Well," Malcolm said, "I've changed my mind about what I said this afternoon. I think you ought to tell your papa what we saw, lad."

Thomas picked up a pair of dice from the game table and tossed them from one hand to the other. "What if we're wrong?" he said. "Maybe he doesn't treat the servants like that. Maybe he thought we were strangers and didn't belong on the homestead at all."

Malcolm rolled his eyes.

"Well, what do I say?" Thomas cried. "'Papa, you and Clayton don't know what you're doing'? Or 'You've hired a monster to run the plantation'?"

"Something like that," Malcolm said.

Thomas dumped the dice miserably on the table. "I don't know. I don't know what I'm supposed to do."

Just then there were voices in the hall, voices that stopped everyone's mouths and made them look anxiously at the door.

"Master wants to talk to all of you in the drawing room right away!" a voice bellowed—too loudly for the narrow area outside the sitting room.

"Why?" said a voice Thomas recognized as Mattie's. "Is something amiss?"

"Just do as I say!" the man barked back.

"But if we've displeased Master Hutchinson in some way, I'd like to know—"

"You'll know soon enough! Now get them together or you'll be talking to the end of a whip!"

And then, as clearly as if it were happening right in the sitting room, there was the sharp crack of flesh hitting flesh. Someone had been slapped.

here was a gasp in the hallway and the sound of boots retreating down the hall. No one moved in the sitting room until the boots were silent.

"That's all the proof I need," Malcolm said. His face was pinched tight with anger.

"He hit her!" Caroline cried. "He hit that sweet Mattie!"

She flew to the door, but when she got it open, there was no one in the hall.

"She's gone to do what she was told," Malcolm said bitterly. "And who can blame her?"

"I wouldn't do it!" Caroline said, hands on hips. "I would go to Master Hutchinson straightaway and tell him!"

"If she doesn't, I know someone who should," Malcolm said. He looked right at Thomas.

Thomas folded his arms and tucked his hands into his armpits. "All right," he said. "I guess I'll have to."

"You can go now, before the meeting," Malcolm said.

"I wonder what that's all about?" Caroline asked. "Can

41

you find that out, too, Tom, while you're at it?"

It was Thomas's turn to roll his eyes. With Malcolm, it was missions. With Caroline, it was secrets and adventures. She couldn't resist them. As he walked miserably out into the hall and went toward his father's library, Thomas wished that for once they would both just be like Patsy and be quiet.

It's easy for them to say, "go talk to Papa," he thought as he crossed the entrance hall. *It's not* their *father they're saying hired the wrong person. It's not* their *father who tells them not to tell tales. It's not* their *father who's going to give them The Look and say, "Thomas, I know your intentions are good, but are you sure you aren't imagining this?"*

He was confused, and whenever he was confused he'd learned that the thing to do was pray. But he wasn't sure what to pray. What was it Papa had said about a bridge?

As he turned to go under the staircase to Papa's library, the door opened and Papa himself came out—with Dawson Chorley behind him. Without quite knowing why, Thomas ducked into the shadows under the stairs.

"I don't want to frighten them," Papa was saying. "But I want them to be aware that there is the possibility of attack by Arnold and that I want no heroes here risking their lives to save the plantation. Most of these people have been with my family since I was born, or before. They are far more important than the outbuildings or the silver—"

"I couldn't agree with you more, sir," Dawson said.

His voice was as smooth as Papa's velvet waistcoat, and Thomas had to pinch himself to keep from poking his head out from under the steps to see if it was really him.

"Good, then we are of like minds," Papa said. They moved off across the hall. "We must be if you are to run the homestead in my absence."

"I can assure you we are, sir," Dawson said.

No you're not! Thomas wanted to shout.

But they disappeared into the drawing room.

Now what? he thought as he stared at the closed door.

He could go bang on it . . . or wait in Papa's library until he came out . . . or go back and ask Malcolm what to do next. But he didn't do any of them. He whipped off Sam's satin waistcoat and kicked off the silver-buckled shoes, shoving both under the bottom step. He slipped out the back door before the rest of the Fearsome Foursome could come looking for him.

He took the back steps two at a time and at the bottom dug his toes into the deep grass of the homestead lawn. As soon as the cool grass touched his feet, he knew where he was going.

That servant boy who was my age—what was his name? he thought to himself as he flew down the hill toward the river. *Patrick! That's it. I haven't even seen him since I've been here. We used to go to that little cove after dark, and no one ever found out.*

That was where he wanted to be now—where no one could find him. There was so much to sort out.

I have to tell Papa, he thought as he took the last rise before the riverbank. *But it's going to be so hard. He already thinks Red Eyes is "of like mind" with him. Now I have to tell him he's wrong!*

But how? he wondered, stumbling down the bank and plunging his feet into the water. *How am I going to do that?*

But as the cool, inky water of the York washed up to his ankles and then his knees, that hard question and the rest washed away.

This cove is where Sam taught me to swim . . . even though Mama said gentlemen didn't dunk themselves into the water.

This is where Otis taught me how to catch fish . . . even though Esther said a well-bred boy like me would never need to do such a thing.

And this is where Patrick and I built that bridge . . .

Thomas stood straight up, water pouring from the folds of the satin breeches, and peered through the darkness around the little cove. Right over there—that was where they'd put their planks across the water and hammered in their railing with nails Otis had given them.

He sloshed through the water to a place in the cove where two fingers of land jutted out into the river. And there it was, the ramshackle board bridge, just the way they'd left it two autumns ago when it had gotten too cold to come down here anymore, and before he'd been sent off to Williamsburg because no one here could control him.

Thomas waded heavily toward the bridge. It was hard to believe he might still be able to walk across it.

And then he stopped. Someone *was* walking across it. It was someone with strong shoulders and, it looked like, no hair. As Thomas watched, the dark form turned toward him and froze.

"It's all right!" Thomas called out.

He swam the rest of the way over and clambered up the bank and onto the bridge. The figure hadn't moved an inch.

"I said it's all right," Thomas repeated as he moved closer. "It used to be my bridge—my friend's and mine—but I haven't used it in a long time."

In the darkness, the man stared at him out of eyes with

whites brighter than the moon. The rest of his face was so black that Thomas could barely see him. With all of his hair shaved off, it was hard to tell where his head ended and the night began. The only other white thing on him was the piece of cloth he had wrapped around him like a pair of short pants.

"Do you work for us now, too?" Thomas asked. "For John Hutchinson?"

The man, whom Thomas saw now couldn't be much older than Malcolm, shook his head so hard that the sweat on his forehead splashed onto Thomas's face. The whites of his eyes flashed again, as if he were terrified.

"Well, that's all right," Thomas said quickly. "My father doesn't mind other people being on his property."

Thomas suddenly felt as if he were talking to a little child. He wasn't sure he'd seen even Patsy look this scared.

"My friend—his name's Patrick," Thomas said. "We built this bridge together. I've been gone a while. I'm surprised it's still standing!"

"It was broke."

Thomas looked at the young man in surprise. His voice was low-pitched, almost like he was singing the words.

"It was?" Thomas said.

The black boy nodded. "I fixed it."

"Why?"

The boy took a step backward as if he were going to bolt from the bridge.

"It's all right!" Thomas said hurriedly. "I just wondered— since it's nothing to you—why you'd take the trouble."

The young man didn't answer. He just moved out on the bridge a little into the moonlight and pointed up to the sky. Thomas didn't look in that direction. He was staring at the man's neck, which was suddenly shining under the moon. He was wearing a tight silver collar with a large letter L engraved into it.

He barely has any clothes on and he's wearing a silver collar? Thomas thought. *How strange.*

When Thomas didn't answer, the young man dropped his hand and began to back away.

"What were you pointing to?" Thomas asked.

"The Lord."

Thomas stared up at the sky over the river, half expecting to see a large face looking down. What he saw were the remains of the sunset, now just purple and silver tendrils in the darkening sky.

"You can see the Lord best from here," the boy said.

"Oh," Thomas said. He studied the sunset as it disappeared into night.

"I didn't mean no harm. I wasn't runnin' away or nothin'. I just wanted to see the Lord tonight."

"Why would you be running away?" Thomas asked. "Are you in trouble?"

Again the black boy shook his head fearfully.

"I told you it was all right to be here," Thomas said.

"Then you won't tell or nothin'?"

"No!" Thomas said. "Who would I tell? I don't even know your name. Who are you?"

For a minute, it looked as if he were going to tell Thomas. His whitened eyes grew softer, and he almost smiled.

But then the bushes on the bank rustled, and the boy coiled like a snake.

"It's probably just a frog or something," Thomas said. "Who are you?"

But the boy had started backing away again, and he stopped at the other end of the bridge only long enough to whisper, "No one." And then he was gone.

Thomas leaned over the rickety railing and strained to see him as he sank into the darkness and disappeared soundlessly into the brush. *Did he mean his name is No One or that he is no one?* Thomas thought.

"No One!" Thomas hollered. "Come back! It's all right!"

"Who are you talking to, Master Thomas?" said a voice behind him. "Who's out there?"

Thomas whirled around with his heart already pounding its way up his throat. Dawson Chorley stood at the other end of the bridge, his arms folded suspiciously across his barrel chest. His eyes squinted down the bridge as his mouth tightened into a line. Thomas glanced nervously into the brush to be sure "No One" was gone. A shudder went through him.

"No one," Thomas said. "I was just . . . I was praying . . . out loud."

"A very fine thing to be doing, Master Thomas," Chorley said. "But then, I would expect nothing less from the son of one of Virginia's finest gentlemen."

Thomas peered at him through the shadows. His eyes were wide and sincere.

"But may I give you a bit of advice, Master Thomas?" he said.

Thomas shrugged.

"I would suggest that you stay close to the house, especially at night. Your father has just informed us all that Benedict Arnold and his men may not be far away—"

"I know," Thomas cut him off sharply. It was strange, but he wasn't afraid of this big, ugly man anymore. As long as

Thomas was John Hutchinson's son, this man wasn't going to do anything to him.

"Good, then," Dawson said, without letting the smile slip from his face. "I am, of course, going to do all I can to protect the homestead in your father's absence."

Not if I tell him what I heard tonight, Thomas thought. The idea of informing on Dawson Chorley was sounding easier in his mind. *And maybe I'll do it . . . first thing tomorrow.*

He turned on his heel to walk away.

"I hope you enjoy the rest of your visit here," Dawson said to his back. "If there is anything I can do to make your stay more pleasant—"

Leave, Thomas thought. He shrugged and went his way.

Thomas was out of bed the next morning, dressed, and on the morning porch having the first of several sugar muffins before the rest of the Fearsome Foursome were up. If he could get Papa alone at breakfast, perhaps he would tell him about Dawson Chorley and get it over with.

But it was Mattie who joined him with fresh milk and a bowl of Cookie's sweet mush. She nodded a polite "Good morning" as she filled his mug. Thomas saw that her hand was shaking.

"What's the matter?" he asked her.

She looked up sharply and splashed milk onto the table. She trembled harder as she set the pitcher down and mopped at the spill with her apron.

"Nothing, Master Thomas," she said. "Just a little clumsy is all."

"Oh," said Thomas. "I know about that. I trip over things all the time."

She stared at him, and then she shifted her eyes away.

I'd be acting skittish, too, if I were working for that mongrel dog Chorley.

Like the snapping of fingers, Thomas had an idea. What if he could get Mattie to tell Papa with him? Then it wouldn't be so hard, and Papa would be more likely to believe him. His father had said it himself—these people were important to him.

"So, Mattie," he said as she anxiously smoothed her apron down and picked up the tray. "What do you think of the new overseer? Chorley . . . isn't that his name?"

The tray clattered to the floor, and Mattie stared down at it in horror. Thomas jumped to pick it up, and then Mattie stared at *him*.

Then the door squeaked open and Papa appeared.

"Good morning, Thomas. Mattie."

Mattie nodded and dodged him with her eyes. She snatched up the tray and said, "I'll go and get your tea, sir."

"You'd better make that two," he said. "We've a visitor coming up the road already . . . and it looks like our neighbor Carter Ludwell." He grinned at Mattie. "Find some sugar for his. He needs all the sweetening up we can manage."

Mattie nodded again and skittered off like a squirrel.

"Mattie must not be feeling well this morning," Papa said. "Did she seem all right to you?"

Now's your chance, Thomas told himself. *Tell him why Mattie isn't all right.*

"Papa," he said slowly, "would you ever hit one of your servants—for any reason?"

Papa frowned a frown so deep that Thomas could feel its pinch. "I am not a slave master like Carter Ludwell, who is this minute coming up our drive," he said. "I have servants whose families have been in the loyal employ of this homestead for generations. I can think of no reason to ever strike any of them." He scowled at the sound of the approaching hoofbeats. "Though I'm sure Mr. Ludwell could suggest several."

"Mr. Ludwell owns slaves?" Thomas asked.

"He has for a long time. He and most of the other planters claim they can't survive without slave labor." Papa grunted. "Tobacco has made slaves of them all."

Mattie came in, and Papa took the teacup she offered him. "Why did you ask me such a question, Thomas?"

Thomas looked warily at Mattie. Her hand was trembling harder than ever as she emptied the rest of the tray.

"I just wondered, sir," he said. He changed his mind about dragging Mattie into this. She would probably faint dead on the floor. Maybe later he could talk to Papa—after Carter Ludwell was gone.

Mr. Ludwell was a Loyalist, and he'd caused a lot of trouble for Papa since the war had started. Even though John Hutchinson's job in Williamsburg was to protect the Loyalists from angry Patriots, Carter Ludwell still thought Papa was trying to run him out of Virginia. A visit from him could only mean an argument that Thomas didn't want to listen to.

A cloud of dust announced their neighbor's arrival, just as the door squeaked open again and Caroline and Patsy appeared on the porch from inside the house. They were dressed in more loose gowns given by the servant children.

"Sugar muffins!" Caroline cried. "Yum! They smell delicious."

"Take some, and we'll have a picnic out under the trees," Thomas said, snatching up several and dumping four more into Caroline's arms.

Caroline blinked at him, but Patsy giggled happily and took an armful and headed for the steps that led to the yard. Her path was blocked by a tight-faced man in more ruffles than would ever be worn by Sam, Clayton, and Papa put together.

"Get out of my way, girl!" Ludwell barked at Patsy. "I have business here. Move on, now!"

Patsy froze and looked up at him helplessly.

"Good heavens, get out of my *way!*" he shrieked.

He shoved her roughly to the side with both hands. Sugar muffins scattered in all directions, and Carter Ludwell stomped on one as he made his way up the steps to the porch. Below him, Patsy was paralyzed with terror.

"Hutchinson!" he squalled. "Can't you teach your servants better manners?"

But it was Carter Ludwell's turn to be shoved. John Hutchinson sent him reeling with the back of his hand and took the steps in one stride getting to Patsy. She was still clutching a sugar muffin as he scooped her up into his arms.

"Are you all right, my dear?" he said. "No need to be afraid now. I have you. Are you all right?"

Patsy finally nodded, but Papa gave her the once-over with his eyes before he set her down. He chucked her lightly under the chin.

"Why don't you run in and ask Mattie for some more of those muffins, eh?" he said.

Patsy smiled up at him as if he had not only saved her from humiliation, but had made the sun come up that morning as well. She skipped off happily to the kitchen building just as Malcolm emerged from it. Thomas exchanged glances with Caroline, and he knew she was thinking just what he was: If Malcolm had witnessed that scene, there would be very little left of Carter Ludwell.

As it was, Carter wasn't going to fare very well. John Hutchinson's face was smoldering.

"What do you mean by such behavior, Ludwell?" Papa said, his voice teetering on the edge of rage.

"She's a servant girl," Carter said "standing there brazen as a—"

"In the first place," Papa cut in, "she is not a servant girl. She is a guest in my home, and even if she were, she is a child—and a human being. We do not treat other human beings as if they were oxen here, not the way you do."

Papa waved an angry arm toward Carter Ludwell's horses, which were stomping nervously at the foot of the front steps.

It was only then that Thomas saw that there was a person standing between them, holding their reins. He could see that he was strong, shaven, and black, and he wore only loose breeches of Ludwell purple and a silver collar around his neck.

"No One!" Thomas whispered.

The boy couldn't have heard him, but he chose that moment to step out from between the horses. Thomas gasped.

Down the broad back was an angry-looking red gash.

Beside him now, Malcolm gasped, too.

"What's the matter?" Caroline whispered.

"That slave," Malcolm said. "He's been beaten with a whip."

✞ ✞ ✞

Chapter Five

Caroline plastered both hands over her mouth.

"Is there no end to the cruelty here?" Malcolm asked.

But Thomas couldn't say a word. He could only stare at the fiery, swollen lash across No One's back.

No One suddenly turned, and his gaze clinked against Thomas's. Thomas wanted to hurdle the porch railing and run to him. *"That boy needs soapwort for the cuts and a dovesdung plaster for the swelling,"* Francis Pickering would have said. No One ducked his head and looked away. Pain seared right through Thomas's middle.

He's ashamed, he thought. *And he probably didn't even do anything wrong!*

"Let's take our breakfast someplace else, shall we?" Malcolm said. "I can't look at this anymore."

They collected Patsy and took their milk and sugar muffins out to a white birch whose limbs dipped to the ground and made a canopy for the Foursome.

Malcolm dropped to the grass and tore savagely at a

muffin. "That slave owner—he's the one who should be whipped!" he said.

"The slave boy," Caroline said to Thomas. "What's his name?"

Thomas looked up quickly from his mug. "I don't know!"

"Oh." Caroline tugged a few crumbs off her muffin and munched thoughtfully. "He looked at you as if he knew you. I thought maybe you'd played together when you were little."

Malcolm snorted loudly. "Played? I bet they had the lad workin' before he could even stand up!"

"Then why did he look at you that way?" Caroline coaxed.

Thomas sighed. "I met him last night. I went down to the bridge that Patrick and I built a while back, and he was there."

"Did he tell you his name?" Caroline asked.

"Bridge?" Patsy asked. "Can we go there?"

"Who's Patrick?" Malcolm asked.

Thomas put his hands over his ears. "I feel like I'm in court before the magistrates!" he said.

"But Tom," Caroline said, "this could lead to something."

"We have a mission, remember?" Malcolm said.

"Can we get that Carter man fired, too?" Patsy said. She shivered. "He's as mean as that Dawson person!"

Thomas looked at them for a minute, all sitting straight up with fire in their eyes.

They'd fight for anything they thought was right, he decided. *I ought to be grateful for that.*

"When I asked him who he was, he said, 'No One,'" Thomas told them. "So that's what I'm calling him. The bridge is down on the cove, and we can go there tonight if you want. And Patrick is one of the servant boys I used to play with. Only I haven't seen him. I don't even know if he's still here."

"What does he look like?" Caroline said. "We'll keep our

eyes open for him."

Thomas had to grin. Her eyes were alive with excitement, and all of the dimples were going at full speed.

"He's smaller than me," Thomas said.

"Who isn't?" Malcolm said dryly.

"And he has a lot of freckles. They stand out when he gets scared."

"He should be easy to spot," Caroline said. "What next?"

"Have you told your father about Old Red Eyes yet?" Malcolm said.

Two of the long, droopy branches were suddenly parted. A large head was thrust into their quiet tent.

"Oh," said Dawson Chorley. His red-rimmed eyes switched from daggers to velvet gloves. "It's our guests again!" The eyes flickered over their clothes. "I see our servants' children have been generous with their garments."

"They're much more comfortable for playing in than our stuffy old fancy clothes," Caroline said. Thomas could see her forcing her smile up to her earlobes. She held out the loose mattress-ticking dress she was wearing. "I'm thinking of dressing like this all the time when I go back to Williamsburg. What about you, Patsy?"

Patsy looked a little bewildered. She *did* dress like that all the time.

"Was there something you wanted, Mr. Chorley?" Caroline said.

Thomas rolled his eyes at Malcolm, who was stifling a grin. Caroline, they knew, was having a wonderful time.

"No," Dawson said. "I was looking for a lazy young servant boy . . . but I haven't found him here, have I?"

They all shook their heads.

"What will you do when you find him?" Caroline asked. "Will you whip him the way Mr. Ludwell did his boy?"

Dawson looked at her sharply, and for a moment Thomas thought the meanness would come back into his eyes. But he nodded politely and said, "I beg your pardon, Mistress—"

"Taylor," she said primly.

"I beg your pardon, Mistress Taylor," Dawson said, "but Mr. Ludwell's boy is a slave, and he caught him trying to run away last night. My young man is only trying to escape his responsibilities, not the whole plantation."

"Trying to run away?!" Thomas cried. The words had come out before he could stop them, and he could feel the hair standing up on the back of his neck in a way it hadn't done in a long time—the way it did when he was angry.

"That's what Mr. Ludwell said," Dawson said. "His overseer caught him down by the river, ready to make his escape."

"That's not true!" Thomas said.

Malcolm shot him a warning look, and Thomas chomped down on his lip. But it hadn't gotten by Dawson Chorley. He narrowed his eyes as he looked at Thomas.

"May I give you another piece of advice, Master Thomas?" he said, as if he were measuring every word with a spoon.

Thomas didn't answer.

"It's best not to interfere with a man and the way he handles his property."

When no one said a word, Dawson nodded his molasses-keg head and backed out of the tree canopy.

"Good morning to you, then," he said coolly, and strolled off across the lawn.

Malcolm let him get out of earshot before he exploded.

"Property?! He called No One Carter Ludwell's property!

Do you see why I want freedom so much?"

"Can we help No One?" Caroline asked.

Malcolm shook his head bitterly. "No. It's still the law that a person can *own* another person."

"But we can help Mattie and the others," Thomas said.

"Go to your father now, lad," Malcolm said. "He'll want to know, so he can put that villain out on the high road and find someone else."

Thomas pushed a couple of limp branches aside and looked up at the house. Carter Ludwell was mounting his horse with No One's help and talking over his shoulder to Papa. No One got up onto the other horse, his back gleaming with sweat. Thomas could feel its salty sting in the gaping wound, and he winced with him. No One hung his head as he followed Mr. Ludwell down the road.

"I'll go talk to Papa," Thomas said. "Meet me in the woodshed."

They all nodded eagerly and slipped out between the leaves. Thomas headed for the house, rehearsing a speech in his head.

Papa, you must get rid of Dawson Chorley. He screams at the servants and hits them.

And Papa would say, *How do you know this?*

He screamed at us when he thought *we were servants. So surely he must treat the others the same way. And we heard him hit Mattie.*

Did you see it?

Well, no, but . . .

And then Papa would give him The Look.

Thomas shook his head. He couldn't think about that.

Besides, he told himself, *at least Papa won't beat me.* If

No One could survive being lashed with a whip, surely he could stand Papa's eyes.

Thomas had taken only the bottom two steps when the front door burst open. Mama was clutching her dressing gown around her, and her gray eyes were wild.

"Thomas, there you are!" she cried. "Where are the others—Malcolm and the girls?"

Something in the way her skin was stretched tight across her face told Thomas not to stall.

"They're in the woodshed," he said. "What's wrong, Mama?"

But she turned to look back into the house and said, "The woodshed, Mattie. Send someone, quickly!"

"I'll get them, Mama," Thomas said, "but why—?"

"No, Thomas, you come inside!" Mama said.

Virginia Hutchinson seldom barked orders, but she was doing it now, and Thomas took the rest of the steps without arguing. She pulled him into the house, slamming the door and bolting it behind him.

"What is it, Mama?" he said.

She pressed him close to her, her tiny hands gripping his big shoulders. "Mr. Ludwell just brought word that one of General Cornwallis's officers was at his plantation last night. The general is tired of chasing Lafayette about, and he's joined Benedict Arnold in ravaging Virginia. Now General Clinton has sent men down from the north—"

The words seemed to hang up in her throat.

"*What*, Mama?" Thomas said.

She shook his shoulders. "We're surrounded, Thomas!" she said. "There are British all around us!"

Thomas knew he was staring at her. This couldn't be real. But the back door burst open and suddenly it was. Papa stomped across the entrance hall with Dawson Chorley at his heels.

"According to Carter Ludwell," Papa was saying, "it's pointless for us to try to escape. We are going to have to turn the mansion into a fortress. Do you understand? I want every man working on nailing shutters closed and securing the bolts. Every woman and child is to be within these walls in 10 minutes' time. Mattie and Cookie have already been assigned to bring in food from the kitchen building."

"Will there be enough room here in the mansion, sir?" Dawson asked. "Perhaps the servants can stay in the barn."

Papa paused and studied Dawson's face. Thomas held his breath.

"I want everyone in the house," John Hutchinson said flatly. "Everyone."

"Yes, sir." Dawson nodded and marched back out the door. Mattie scurried across the hall toward the dining room, her arms piled high with bowls and pie tins. A young servant girl darted out from the drawing room and curtsied, unseen, to Mama as she raced through.

"I'm fetchin' more linens," she called to Mattie.

Papa turned to Mama and took her face in both hands.

"Not to worry, my dear. Are you praying?"

"Are you sure about this, John? Perhaps Carter Ludwell was lying to you."

"He offered to tell the British we were devout Loyalists— if I would pay him."

"Wretched man!"

"My words precisely, my dear," Papa said. "We are Patriots, and we will behave as such." He looked at Thomas. "Where are the others?"

"Here, sir!" Malcolm said from the back door. "What would you have me do?"

"And me, too, Papa," Thomas said.

Papa nodded. "Malcolm, you see that the third floor is battened down. Thomas, help Mattie bring in firewood. We'll use the fireplace in the dining room for cooking."

"Girls, come with me," Mama said to Caroline and Patsy. "I'm sure we can be of some help with the kitchen things."

The afternoon sped by with no time for Thomas to stop and ask himself, *Is this real? Is this really happening?*

Every time he passed Caroline, she had a gleam of adventure in her eyes that told him it wasn't. But the dark concentration in Malcolm's eyes shouted that it was indeed real. By the time the wood was piled high in the hallway outside the dining room and the drawing room was lined with pallets for the servants to sleep on and the house was darkened by its tightly fastened shutters, Thomas's heart was pounding with how very real it was. The look on his father's face when he gathered everyone in the parlor sent it right up into his throat.

"It may very well be that Arnold and Cornwallis will both pass us by," Papa said. "The house can't be seen from the river, and we've done a little harmless damage at the edges of the land to make them think from their boats that this property has already been hit." He nodded toward Dawson. "Thanks to Mr. Chorley's cleverness."

"Sir?" Malcolm said. "What about Lafayette? Isn't he in Virginia with a company of soldiers? Might he not be headin' off the British?"

"Perhaps," Papa said, "but he hasn't had his men together long enough for them to be battle-wise yet."

"So we could very well be attacked here," Dawson said.

Reluctantly, Papa nodded. "We could be. But we're ready. And as long as everyone follows certain rules, we should all come out quite safely. Arnold's men want supplies, and they want to leave their mark. They are welcome to do both as far as I am concerned, as long as none of you is hurt."

He looked at all of them solemnly. "I want no one leaping from the house to save a horse or salvage a side of salt pork. We will not burn candles or shed any other kind of light unless there is an emergency. Obviously, we will want to stay as quiet as possible."

No one seemed to be able to do anything but nod.

Papa smiled a little. "This would all be something of a prison sentence if it weren't for Cookie. She has prepared a feast, which you are welcome to help yourselves to at any time in the dining room. That should sweeten the prospect, eh?"

There was a chorus of satisfied grunts and ahs.

Thomas stole a look at Dawson.

But Dawson was nodding along with the rest, and he even reached over and squeezed Mattie's hand as if to reassure her. Mattie stared at it and pulled her hand away as soon as he let go.

The 30 or so servants milled about uncertainly for a moment as if they didn't know where to go in the big house. All except Malcolm, who hissed to Thomas from across the room and motioned for him to follow him into the sitting room. Thomas wriggled through the crowd and slid out of the crowded hall and into the room where they'd met last night. He turned, expecting to find only Patsy and Caroline with him. But standing awkwardly next to the game table was a lanky boy with auburn hair and a multitude of freckles from forehead to foot.

Thomas stared at him for a full minute before he said, "Patrick?"

The boy's neck was so thin that Thomas could see his Adam's apple as he gulped.

"Yes, sir," Patrick said.

Thomas blinked. "Sir? You never called me sir before!"

"What did he call you?" Caroline said.

"A big, clumsy oaf, mostly," Thomas said, grinning. "Why are you calling me sir?"

"Probably because you beat the stuffing out of him last time you saw him," said Malcolm. His eyes were dancing. "At least that's what he told us."

"No," Patrick said. "I do it because Mr. Chorley told me I should—out of respect."

"Oh," Caroline said. "Did he tell you to lick his boots, too?"

Patrick looked around a little wildly, and his freckles began to stand out on his pale face.

"Never mind, Patrick," Thomas said. "And you don't have to call me sir. I don't care what that Mr. Chorley says."

"That isn't the half of it," Malcolm said. He slipped into a chair and nudged Patrick. "Sit down and tell Thomas what you told us this morning in the woodshed."

"That's where we found him hiding from Mr. Chorley," Caroline put in.

"Did you steal some shrewsbury cakes from the pantry?" Thomas asked him. "You always got into trouble for that."

They all looked at Patrick, who sank miserably into a chair and studied his boot tops. "I'm workin' harder than I ever worked before," he said finally. "But Mr. Chorley says I'm lazy! He says I run off every time there's work to be done!"

"But he doesn't!" Caroline said. "He only goes to the

woodshed to rest when he's so tired he can't hold his head up anymore!"

"And this morning I went there because he told Mattie he was coming after me with a whip to get me going on my morning chores. Mattie's my cousin," he said to Caroline, "so of course she came and told me."

"You don't have to worry much longer," Thomas said. "I have some things to tell Papa about Dawson Chorley, and I think after that he'll be gone. Only . . ." He stopped and sighed. "Only I haven't had a chance yet, what with all this going on."

"And besides," Caroline said, "Chorley always acts like a nursemaid to all of you whenever Mr. Hutchinson is looking. He won't do anything to you with everyone here under the same roof."

Patrick looked a little relieved, but he still shot Thomas a cautious look. "Why are you being so nice to me?"

Thomas frowned. "Why wouldn't I be?"

But Patrick was shaking his head. "You weren't always nice to me—just before you left. You're different now."

Thomas squirmed inside his shoulders. Why did everyone keep saying that? He wasn't that different, he didn't think. This called for a change of subject. "Did you know that bridge we built in the cove is still there?" he said brightly.

Patrick shook his head. "I haven't been down there since Mr. Chorley came."

"'Mr. Chorley,'" Caroline said thoughtfully. "That's too good for him. Why don't you try 'Old Red Eyes'? That's what we all call him."

Patsy giggled and Malcolm managed a chuckle, and before long even Patrick was smiling. He only smiled with one side of his mouth, Thomas remembered that now. He used to do it just before he said, "Big, clumsy oaf" . . . just before Thomas punched him.

Thomas shook himself and said, "Is anybody hungry?"

They grazed around the dining room table and took their plates back to the sitting room. Malcolm, Patsy, and Caroline listened as if they were in a trance while Thomas and Patrick told stories of growing up on the homestead. When they went back to the dining room to see if there was any dessert left, everyone seemed to be drifting off to bed. Papa and Dawson sat in chairs at the doors, and Papa urged them to get some rest.

"No one's to sleep out in the servants' hall," Thomas said to Malcolm and Patrick. "Why don't you come up and sleep in my room?"

"You'll be right across the hall from us," Caroline said as she took Patsy's hand. "Maybe we'll wake you up for a midnight snack!"

As he lay across his bed with Malcolm and Patrick sprawled out on either side of him, Thomas had to force himself to remember this wasn't a party. Except for the stifling heat from being in the house with all the shutters nailed down, there was little to remind him that they were waiting for the British to invade the homestead. He had his friends around him, and he was happy . . . until just after midnight, when he was awakened by a scream from across the hall.

‡ ‧‡‧ ‡

Chapter Six

Thomas's eyes sprang open. The scream came again. Patrick groaned, and Malcolm bolted up.

"Patsy!" he cried.

He tore across both Thomas and the still-moaning Patrick. Thomas sprang after him and caught the door as Malcolm flung it open. They both froze in the doorway as the girls' door opened across the hall and a dark form was silhouetted in the frame. Their room was alive with light that flickered and wavered in the breeze coming in through the window.

Thomas's thoughts pawed through the cobwebs of sleep.

Their window is open.

Someone has a firebrand lighting up their room.

Somebody is coming out their door.

And from the screams and kicks, Thomas knew that somebody was trying to hold Patsy.

Thomas could see her being held by a wide man in a scarlet waistcoat. His brass buttons glittered in the torch fire someone else was carrying.

Malcolm plowed headfirst into the stomach of the soldier who held Patsy and knocked him backward a step. Malcolm tried to wrench Patsy away, but the soldier reached behind him with his free arm and, with a slicing sound that cut the air, produced his sword. He swung it menacingly over his head and brought Malcolm and Thomas to a frozen halt.

"Get back!" the soldier shouted at them.

He stared them down with stone-cold blue eyes until their backs were against wall in the hallway. Thomas could feel Malcolm's chest heaving.

"What are you going to do to her?" Malcolm shouted.

"Shut it!" said the soldier. The dark-brown chops of hair on his cheeks rippled like reptiles. "You, too!" he said, giving Patsy a shake. She put her hand over her mouth and cried silently. Thomas felt as if he were going to be sick.

"Dickinson!" the soldier shouted into the girls' room. "Haven't you got that other one under control yet?"

For answer, the wide soldier who held Caroline yelped like a dog. "She bit me!" he cried.

"Good!" Malcolm said. "You deserve it!"

He made a move to lunge at the soldier in the hall again, but before he got an inch, the sword whooshed down and stabbed through the loose fold of Malcolm's shirt and into the wall. He was pinned there like a notice nailed to a message board. His dark face went scarlet.

"You'll get the same if you make a move," the soldier spat at Thomas.

Thomas's heart was pounding so hard that he could only flatten himself against the wall.

"What are you going to do to her?" Malcolm said through his teeth. "You'd better not hurt her!"

"We're not going to hurt her if everyone does just exactly as we say," the soldier said. He smiled an ugly, yellow-toothed smile. "We've been told you have upwards of 30 people in this house, all clinging to the master like a bunch of piglets on a sow. There's only a handful of us against all of you." He shook a whimper out of Patsy. "We need a wee bit of assurance that we'll get everything we need."

From inside the room, Caroline let out a shriek loud enough to wake the dead.

Why doesn't it wake Papa or Dawson? Thomas thought. *Why doesn't someone come?*

"We'll just walk down the stairs with these two, and our men can do the rest." He revealed his stained teeth again.

"How is having these girls going to stop the master and his men from taking you on?" Malcolm said bitterly. "You don't know who you're facing down there—"

"Oh, yes, I do," Muttonchops said smugly. "Mr. Ludwell was kind enough to tell us that Mr. Hutchinson will do anything—if we're holding a gun to his children's heads!"

Malcolm ripped his shirt away from the wall, bringing the sword crashing to the floor, and shot his arms around the soldier, Patsy and all.

"What's happening?" cried Dickinson from inside the room.

He bolted for the doorway, and Caroline squirmed away from him. She dove to the floor and crawled out after him. The soldier with the firebrand was right behind her.

Thomas exploded into action. He leaned over and scooped up the sword that lay at his feet and thrust it toward the soldier who was chasing Caroline. It caught on something—the soldier yipped—and Caroline wriggled around him, and around Dickinson, who was trying to peel Malcolm away, and around Muttonchops, who was still struggling to hold on to Patsy while Malcolm pummeled him with his fists.

Once beyond them, she scrambled to her feet and took off down the stairs, screaming, "Mr. Hutchinson! Mr. Hutchinson! Help!"

Thomas stared at the sword in his hand, and then at the soldier leaning against the door frame, trying to hold on to the firebrand and examine his arm at the same time. Thomas couldn't move.

"Get off him!" Dickinson was screaming at Malcolm as he fought to tear him away. "I'll run you through!"

Thomas watched helplessly as the wide soldier groped behind him for his sword. Muttonchops shifted Patsy to one hip and got a shot in at Malcolm's eye. Thomas heard him groan, but he could only stand and watch, with a blood-tipped sword in his hand.

"Thomas!" someone hissed behind him. "Over here!"

Thomas willed himself to look around. Patrick had come to life in the doorway to Thomas's room, and he was nodding his head furiously toward Dickinson. The fat soldier was sweating through his scarlet waistcoat and breathing like a worn-out horse.

Patrick nodded again, and Thomas suddenly knew what to do. Still clutching the sword, he made a dive for Dickinson's back. Patrick dove, too, and together they wrestled the gasping man to the floor. He was heavy in his blubbery state, but he was too tired to fight back much. Patrick had no trouble planting his foot in the middle of the soldier's chest. He motioned for Thomas to put the sword to his throat.

Without Dickinson on his back, Malcolm took a free swing and caught Muttonchops in the stomach. He gasped, and his hands shot out. Patsy slid to the floor with a thud.

"Run, Patsy!" Thomas cried. "Run down the stairs."

But she clung to the floor and looked up at Malcolm. He was struggling to keep Muttonchops's head down. One more blow and Malcolm would have him on the floor.

"Run, Patsy!" Thomas shouted again. "Malcolm is all right—run down the stairs."

Still she lay rooted to the floor, until an idea flashed in Thomas's head. "Go find my father!" he told her. "Go find Mr. Hutchinson!"

That seemed to jar her loose. She scrambled to her feet and turned to run for the stairs. Dickinson made no move to challenge Thomas's sword, and Malcolm at last hacked Muttonchops in the back with his forearm and dropped him to the floorboards.

"We did it!" Thomas cried to Patrick.

But Patrick looked over Thomas's shoulder, and his eyes flew open. Thomas whirled around in time to see the soldier with the firebrand hurl himself past all of them toward the stairs. In three strides of his long legs, he scooped up Patsy and held her by the middle, upside down, and brandished the flaming club above them all.

"We have her, men!" he cried. "This is all we need!"

For the first time, Thomas saw that this soldier he had nicked on the arm with the sword was barely as old as Malcolm. His golden eyes were swimming, and Thomas could see his lips trembling like he was holding back tears. He jiggled Patsy as if she were a rabbit he'd just snagged and tore down the stairs with her, shouting, "Captain! Captain, I have what we need. I have a prisoner!"

Thomas pulled the sword away from Dickinson and ran for the steps. He could feel Malcolm and Patrick on his heels, and he knew Dickinson and Muttonchops were right behind them, but he didn't stop. . . . Not until he reached the turn in the staircase and skidded to a halt as if he'd come up against a wall of fire. On the steps stood a short, sturdy man in white breeches and a scarlet waistcoat that glistened with ribbons and decorations. Below him in the entrance hall, a sea of faces looked up at him, mirroring the horror they felt.

For with one hand he held Caroline around the neck. And in the other hand he held a gleaming pistol, pointed straight at her head.

Firebrand Boy stood beside him, holding Patsy out by the back of her nightshift like a prize and grinning proudly. Patsy was crying so hard that Thomas was sure she didn't even know who she was anymore.

"Good work, Knox," the captain said. "You hold on to her in case we need her. All right?"

Knox nodded eagerly. Malcolm tried to lunge for him, but Dickinson caught him from behind by one arm and Muttonchops, still rattling for breath, grabbed him by the other. Then one of them yanked the sword away from Thomas.

"No!" Malcolm screamed. "Let her go!"

"Can't you shut him up?" the captain said without turning around. "I must have quiet if we are to proceed."

Knox continued down the steps, still dangling Patsy. As he watched, Thomas saw a smear of faces at the bottom. Only two stood out. One was Papa's, at the back of the crowd by the front door. He was being held on either side by a pair of red-coated soldiers whose faces matched their uniforms. John Hutchinson was making them work to keep him there.

The other face was right at the bottom of the steps, and it belonged to Dawson Chorley. Even from here, Thomas could see the red rings around the big man's eyes as he watched in rage. There was no one holding his arms.

By now, Knox had reached the bottom step, and he tossed the firebrand over the heads of the Hutchinsons' servants to one of the soldiers who was holding Papa. Then he turned Patsy right side up and held her up.

"We all see her, Knox," the captain said tightly. "Now take her over there to the corner—"

"No!" Malcolm screamed. "Let her go, I say!"

He wrenched one arm away from Dickinson and lurched forward.

The captain turned his head to look up at him. "Can't you keep him in check, Dickinson?" he said.

Dickinson groped to catch hold of Malcolm's arm. The captain watched in disgust, not seeing what Thomas saw below them, behind the captain's back.

Dawson Chorley reached up and snatched Patsy right out of Knox's hands. Before the young man could even yelp, Dawson ducked behind the knot of people and disappeared.

When he could gather himself together, Knox cried, "Captain!"

But the captain whirled around to face the crowd, tightened the gun against Caroline's temple and said tersely, "Let us get on with it, Mr. Hutchinson—"

"But Captain!" cried Knox.

"Shut it!" snapped the captain. With a jerk, he pointed the pistol to the ceiling and cracked the air with a shot. The servants screamed as one and ducked their heads. Thomas picked out Mama, standing upright by the drawing room door with a layer of servants' children wrapped around her. Her face was taut with anger and terror, but she didn't flinch.

"Now let us proceed," the captain said. "Where are the rest of the food supplies, Mr. Hutchinson? We have your horses and a fair amount of salted meats—"

"I said you can have anything you want," John Hutchinson shouted up at him. "There was never any need for any of these dramatics."

"I never saw a man yet that would let go of his belongings freely, without a bit of a nudge, eh?"

The captain tightened the pistol against Caroline's head, and it occurred to Thomas that he hadn't heard her give so much as a whimper.

"I think you'll find everything you need in the kitchen building," Papa said.

"Is that the delicious aroma I have been smelling ever since I arrived?" said the captain.

"Your men can go and see for themselves," Papa said. "Take anything you want, I tell you. I won't fight you."

But the captain shook his head. "No, what I smell is coming from back there." He nodded toward the dining room. "Will one of you gentlemen see to that, please?"

One of the soldiers let go of Papa and worked his way through the crowd to the dining room. He ducked his head in and came out smiling.

"There's a feast awaiting us, Captain!" he said.

"Good," said the captain. "We shall partake before we leave. For now, gentlemen, I think we have convinced Mr. Hutchinson that he and his family and servants will come to no harm if we are allowed to go about our business."

Dickinson and Muttonchops elbowed their way past Malcolm, Thomas, and Patrick, and the crowd below parted to let them through to the front door. The two men guarding Papa unbolted it, and Thomas knew then that all of them had broken in through Patsy and Caroline's window. He could feel the hair standing up on the back of his neck.

The captain stayed on the steps, still holding the pistol to Caroline's head as he watched Papa. The rest of the soldiers headed out the door. Knox whined that someone had taken his prisoner, but one of them told him to "Shut it!" and another one smacked him on the side of the head, and he was finally quiet.

It seemed to take hours for the soldiers to forage through the homestead and take everything they "needed." Dickinson gleefully emerged from the dining room at one point with the two silver candelabra, and the captain nodded his approval.

"What do they need those for?" Patrick whispered.

"They'll get money for them," Malcolm whispered back. "What I want to know is where that cow has taken Patsy!"

Thomas nodded vaguely. All he could think about was the gun pointed at Caroline's head. It was steaming hot there on the stairs. What if the captain's hand grew sweaty and his finger slipped on the trigger?

What if somebody moves suddenly and he jerks and accidentally shoots her? What if Caroline . . . gets killed?

What should I do?

He groped through the crowd below him with his eyes and found Papa again, this time standing in the middle of them, as helpless as Thomas was. Only his father didn't look helpless. His Hutchinson eyes were concerned, but his face looked calm, and his lips were moving silently.

He's praying, Thomas thought. *I should be praying, but what do I pray for? God, help me to . . . do what? I can't do anything!*

Once again, Thomas tried to remember what it was his father had said about a bridge. Thomas fumbled for words and came out with: *God, please be the bridge for Caroline— between what she needs to be safe and what I can do!*

"I think we've got it all, Captain," said Muttonchops. "And plenty from the dining room as well."

"Good. We shall have a feast aboard our boat."

Muttonchops grinned his dingy smile. "Shall I bring you a horse, sir?"

"Well, of course," said the captain. "Our visit wouldn't be complete without it, now, would it?"

Papa parted the knot of servants with his arm and moved to the bottom of the stairs. "Since you're preparing to ride out of here," he said to the captain, "will you set the little girl free? The poor child is frightened to death."

Actually, Thomas didn't think Caroline looked frightened at all. The captain had long since slackened his hold on both her and the gun, and she was glaring up at him with her round, brown eyes blazing, as if for two schillings she'd gladly kick him in the shins. Thomas almost wanted to laugh.

"The child has been very cooperative," the captain admitted. "Perhaps she would like to go for a ride with me— as a treat."

The laughter died in Thomas's throat.

"What are you saying, man?" Papa said. His foot went up on the bottom step, and the captain tightened his arm around Caroline's neck. Thomas heard the trigger click.

"I'm saying I've grown somewhat attached to the child. I think she might like to take a little farewell ride with me."

"Your horse is ready, sir," Muttonchops said from the front door.

"You promised there would be no harm done to anyone here!" John Hutchinson shouted.

"No harm will come to her," the captain said calmly. He moved down the staircase with Caroline. "Shall we, my dear?"

"Papa, don't let him!" Thomas cried.

But on the bottom step, Papa shook his head slightly and fixed his eyes on the captain.

"Surely, sir," he said, "you are not planning to carry this child off on a British military vessel—"

"Don't be a fool, man," the captain said as he brushed past Papa, still holding Caroline and the pistol. "I told you, I only want to reward her with a ride."

There was a gasp from the front as both double doors swung open. Muttonchops stepped in—holding Judge by the reins.

"Step aside, if you please!" he sang out.

The servants had no choice but to move away as the soldier led Papa's enormous bay into the central hall.

"John!" Mama cried.

"What is the purpose in this?" John Hutchinson said to the captain.

But the short, sturdy officer didn't answer. He nodded to one of Papa's guards, who hoisted Caroline up into the saddle, and then he mounted the horse himself. Only then did he return the pistol to his holster and smile down at the crowd.

"Ladies and gentlemen," he said, "I would advise you to move aside. This young lady and I are about to take a ride!"

Almost before anyone had a chance to move, the captain jabbed his heels into Judge's sides and the big horse reared up on his hind legs. People scattered, screaming, into the rooms that opened onto the hall. Only Mama and Papa remained, gaping in disbelief as the captain brought Judge down on all fours and smacked him with his heels again. Judge lurched forward, his eyes wild. The captain jerked him first toward the drawing room, and Mama scurried to Papa's arms. Then he reined him back toward the parlor, and Papa picked up Mama and carried her up the stairs.

At the top, Thomas leaned over the railing and squeezed it with both hands.

"He's a madman!" Malcolm shouted behind him.

Caroline's eyes were wild as she clung to the saddle horn, and there were no dimples in the pale cheeks. The only thing there was stark terror.

"I wouldn't go up the stairs if I were you, Mr. Hutchinson," the captain said as Judge danced frantically at the bottom of the staircase. "Because that's where we're headed!"

Once more, he brought Judge up on his hind legs and let out a shout as if he were going into battle. When the horse's hooves came down on the floor, he backed the horse toward the door and kept his eyes on the top step.

"Get out of the way, gentlemen," he shouted at Thomas, Malcolm, and Patrick. "Lest you be mowed down!"

And without waiting for them to move, he kicked at Judge's sides—and rode the horse straight up the steps.

✢ ⭑ ✢

Chapter Seven

Papa got to them in three strides and shoved Mama and the boys onto the upper landing. "Stop, man!" he shouted down over his shoulder. "You'll break the horse's leg and kill both of you!"

But they watched in horror as the captain continued to drive Judge up the stairs, almost to the top, before he stopped and threw his head back and laughed.

"Are you enjoying your ride, mistress?" he asked Caroline.

"No!" she cried. "I want to get off!"

"All right, then. I suppose we'll have to cut our ride short."

There was an evil smile plastered across the captain's face. He carefully maneuvered a very frightened Judge around and headed him down the stairs. When he reached the bottom, Thomas breathed a sigh.

"Let the girl down now, sir, please," John Hutchinson said. "Your ride is finished."

But to Thomas's horror, the captain reached behind him

and whisked his sword from its scabbard.

"One last turn around the hall, mistress!" he cried.

He pulled out his heels and drove them hard into Judge's ribs. With the sword waving wildly over his head, he set off at a trot along the outer edge of the hall.

"Here's one for King William!" he called out.

He rode past the portrait of Daniel Hutchinson and gave it a swipe with his sword. The blade cut right across the noble painted face of Thomas's grandfather. Then he kicked his heels in again and sailed toward the painting of Joseph and his family.

"And one for Jolly Olde England, eh? What do you say?"

He cut a figure-eight into the air above his head with the sword and leaned toward the painting. Suddenly, Caroline reached up with both hands and yanked at his arm. He slid sideways and the sword clattered to the hall floor. The captain lunged for it, nearly losing his balance.

Caroline clung to Judge's mane and cried out, "Whoa! Whoa, boy!"

Judge came to a grateful halt at the side of the staircase and tossed his head up and down in a fit of panic. Papa was down the stairs and had Caroline off and into his arms before the captain could right himself.

"End this ridiculous game and leave my home at once," Papa said. "You've gotten what you came for and then some."

The captain slid off the horse and tugged importantly at the bottom of his waistcoat. "I will leave when I am ready to leave," he said. He pulled the pistol deftly from its holster—and pointed it at Papa.

John Hutchinson dropped Caroline and gave her a shove. Mama caught her at the bottom of the stairs and held her.

Papa put his hands slowly into the air.

"If you are going to shoot me," he said, "please do it outside. Not in front of all of these—"

The captain laughed and tipped the barrel of the pistol up and shot once more at the ceiling.

"Now I am ready to leave," he said. "And you can keep this horse. He isn't worth his weight in feathers."

With one final flourish of his hand, he was gone. Muttonchops picked up his sword and left behind him.

No one moved until the voices and the hoofbeats faded. And they waited until Papa had looked out the window and reassured them that the soldiers were indeed gone before they crept from their doorways.

It was only then that Caroline began to cry. She pressed her face into Mama's lap, and she didn't stop until long after Papa had carried her into the parlor and laid her on the velvet sofa. Finally, with some chamomile tea from Mattie and the promise from Papa that the British were gone for good, she sat up and squeezed out a dimple or two.

"They have no reason to come back," Papa said. "They've taken everything."

"Not everything," Mama said. She stroked Thomas's hair. "No one was hurt—not even Judge."

"That's right," said Papa. "I had Patrick check him over."

Caroline's face puckered again. "That was the only part that scared me," she said. "I knew he wouldn't really shoot me. His hand was so steady when he held the gun." She shivered, and the tears pooled in her eyes. "But when he started riding the horse up the stairs, he was shaking all over. I didn't know what he'd do then!"

"Malcolm was right," Papa said. "He was a madman."

Thomas looked around, and Caroline followed his eyes.

"Where is Malcolm?" Caroline said. "And Patsy?"

Thomas's stomach suddenly grew uneasy. Malcolm had left to look for her the minute the British were gone. His parting words had been, "If Dawson Chorley has hurt her, it'll be the last thing he does!"

"I'll look into it," Papa said, and left the room as Mattie appeared with a tray sparsely dotted with a bowl of strawberry preserves, a torn hunk of bread, and a pile of apricots.

"This is all that's left after those devils had their fill," she said. "I heard one of them say the apricots weren't ripe!"

"I guess beggars certainly can be choosers," Mama said. She offered the tray to Caroline. "Since you are our little heroine, you take what you want first."

"Why am I the heroine?" she said.

"Because you kept that insane man from destroying the portrait of the Joseph Hutchinsons." Mama leaned in and lowered her voice. "I know Mr. Hutchinson says that possessions aren't important, but those paintings represent something that is very important to him, and that is his family. I know he's grateful to you, Caroline."

"I liked that painting from the minute I walked into the house—just the way I liked Thomas the first time I saw him."

Thomas felt his face go red, and he squirmed in his chair, crossed and uncrossed his arms, and finally got up and looked out into the hall. To his immense relief, Malcolm was making his way toward him with Patsy enthroned on his back. She smiled her crooked-toothed smile, and Thomas started to grin back at her, when Dawson Chorley rounded the corner behind her with Papa.

They all crowded into the parlor, and everyone chattered

at once until Papa put his big hand up for silence.

He smiled his rare smile. "I don't think any of us will rest until we've all heard Mr. Chorley's story."

Only because it's about Patsy, Thomas thought stubbornly. His anger against the overseer crept back up his backbone again. *Let's hear it now, because tomorrow, you'll probably be gone. I will tell Papa before we go to sleep tonight.*

"Tell us, Dawson," Papa said.

Caroline shot Thomas a look. *So it's "Dawson" now?* her face said.

Thomas shot back a look that said, *I like Old Red Eyes better.*

"Luck was on my side tonight," Dawson Chorley said, bobbing his head modestly. "When that *infant* of a soldier stopped right next to me and was dangling Mistress Patsy here like a carrot in front of a donkey, I couldn't do anything but grab her. And there were so many people crowded into the hall, I saw my chance to sneak her right out of the room. It was obvious that officer was half mad, and there was no telling what he might do to the poor child if he had a chance." He nodded respectfully to Papa. "And I know how important she is to you, sir."

Thomas heard Malcolm sniff quietly. *He's thinking what I'm thinking,* Thomas told himself. *What if Old Red Eyes knew Patsy was only an indentured servant?*

"We slipped down this hall out here," Mr. Chorley was saying. "Then I thought, 'Where would be the safest place to hide this little treasure?'"

Thomas saw Malcolm's eyebrows twitch.

"And then I remembered something I learned from you, Master Thomas."

Thomas looked at him quickly.

"I hope you don't mind," Dawson went on, "but I took her to the cove by the makeshift bridge. But I told her not to get on it, since that bridge is a hazard. I'd like your permission to tear it down, Mr. Hutchinson, sir, as soon as the dust has settled on this."

Thomas started to protest, and then he remembered: *I don't need to worry about the bridge. Dawson Chorley will probably be gone tomorrow.*

"Go on, sir," John Hutchinson said. "Tell them the rest."

"I set to looking around a bit. And lo and behold I could watch it all from right there in that hidden cove!"

"Watch what?" Mama asked.

"Why, those British soldiers loading sacks of your belongings onto their vessel! I must say, I was most distressed when I saw them go aboard with your fine silver candelabra."

"Go on," Papa said. "Tell them what you did, sir."

"I did what any one of you would have done if you had been in my position," he said. "I went to the barn and fetched some empty sacks and stuffed them with straw. Then while they were having their last hoot and holler in the hall . . . what was that all about anyway?"

"Presently," Papa said. "Finish your story."

"Well, during that time, I pulled their sacks off and put mine on. Your supplies are in the brush down by the cove, and the British have just made off with a dozen bags of fine straw!"

Thomas saw that his eyes weren't the only ones popping.

"Now, I wasn't able to get everything before I heard them coming back," Mr. Chorley said to Mama. His red-rimmed eyes grew soft as he took her hand. "I'm afraid they got off with your candelabra."

"It doesn't matter!" Mama cried, squeezing his hands in hers. "We're all safe. Isn't that what counts?"

"Indeed it is, my dear," Papa said. "I believe we owe Mr. Chorley a debt of gratitude—not only for saving our Patsy, but for outsmarting the British as well."

Thomas's thoughts were hopelessly tangled. But Malcolm seemed to have his in perfect order.

"Sir," he said to Papa, "didn't you say that none of us were to perform anything heroic to try to save the supplies?"

"Yes, I did. But I can hardly admonish Dawson here for being so clever. He didn't endanger anyone's life in the process, and that is what I was concerned about."

"But what if the British discover what he's done and come back?"

"Begging your pardon, Master Malcolm," Mr. Chorley said, "but they had bags from several other plantations on board as well. I doubt they'll open any of them before they have rejoined their ship, and then it will be impossible to tell which one did the deed. I don't think we have anything more to fear from the British."

Malcolm nodded sullenly and sat back in his chair. Papa stood up and extended his hand to Dawson Chorley.

"I must admit, sir, I had some misgivings about hiring on a man I'd never met. And you did seem stubborn at first. But I think you will do just fine as our overseer in Clayton's absence."

Caroline sat up on the sofa, and Patsy's eyes widened to plate-size. Malcolm gripped the arms of his chair. And all of their eyes were on Thomas.

What do you expect me to do? Thomas thought. His mouth went dry. *I want to stand up now and say, "No, Papa, you're wrong!" But I can't! I can't!*

Even if he could have, the opportunity passed as Papa turned to them all and said, "I think it's best we pray together now and then try to rest. Mr. Chorley and I have much to do tomorrow to restore the plantation to normal, and the rest of you have a journey ahead."

Thomas's head snapped up. "A journey, Papa?"

Papa nodded. "I think it's time you all went back to Williamsburg. No one can argue that it's much safer there!"

"If the British aren't coming back here, what is there to worry about?" Thomas said.

"Those were Cornwallis's men," Papa said. "We've still not seen Benedict Arnold, nor any of Clinton's soldiers, should they take a notion to join in terrorizing Virginia."

"I quite agree, sir," Mr. Chorley said. "What could possibly happen in sleepy little Williamsburg that could compare with what we've seen here tonight?"

Who asked you? Thomas thought. *Now that you're the hero, you're going to start giving Papa advice?*

Evidently so, because Papa clapped him on the shoulder and said, "Mr. Chorley is right. You will head for safer ground tomorrow. Malcolm, I'll ask you to escort the ladies home."

"Yes, sir," he said stiffly.

Papa asked them all to bow their heads in prayer. Thomas tried to pray for another bridge—but he couldn't even put it into words. He looked around the circle instead and saw Malcolm with his eyes open, too. He definitely wasn't praying.

He was glaring at Dawson Chorley with a stare that said, *We'll show them who you really are, sir. We surely will.*

✠ ✠ ✠

Chapter Eight

Caroline and Patsy were far too frightened to go back up to their room, so it was decided that the children—including Patrick—could all sleep in the sitting room.

But as soon as the door was closed, it was Malcolm who started right in.

"So he's a hero now!"

"He made himself sound like George Washington or some such!" Caroline turned to Patsy who was curled up on a pallet beside her. "Was he mean to you?"

"No," she said. "But he didn't treat me like a 'treasure' either. The minute he saw the British loading their boats, he forgot all about me."

That was a lot for Patsy to say, and she burrowed back in close to Caroline.

"That proves it, doesn't it, lads and lassies?"

"But it isn't going to prove it to Papa!" Thomas said. "You aren't still expecting me to tell him, are you? He'll never believe me now!"

Malcolm mulled that over for a minute. "I suppose not." He sighed. "I don't guess there's anything we can do now."

"Still," Caroline said, "I hate to leave Patrick and Mattie and the others with him."

Patrick nodded. His freckles looked an inch thick on his pale skin. "And he's going to be worse than ever with so much work to do, cleaning things up and all."

Caroline nodded sympathetically, and Thomas punched glumly at his pillow. Even Malcolm had to shrug his shoulders. It was a sad group that drifted off to sleep with the sun coming up over the York River.

But at least Thomas thought of a prayer. *Please bridge the gap between what Patrick needs and what we can do for him,* he whispered to God.

"Patrick?" Thomas hissed.

Patrick moaned.

"Don't let Mr. Chorley tear down our bridge."

There was silence, and then Patrick said in a clear voice, "All right, Thomas. I won't."

The sun was on its way toward noon when Mama tapped on the sitting room door and rousted them out. "You must all eat before we leave," she said. "Malcolm, Mr. Hutchinson would like for you to see to Judge."

Thomas sat up and rubbed his eyes sleepily. "How will we pull the carriage with only one horse?" he asked.

Mama smiled. "Our Mr. Chorley even managed to slip Burgess off the boat, and he's gone off to the Fitzhughs to see if he can buy a few more. The Fitzhughs had their buggy stolen last night, so they've no need for all their horses." She sighed. "God has blessed us yet again with this man."

"Now he's not just a hero, he's a blessing," Malcolm muttered after she was gone. "I'm sorry, but he's not one I'll be thankin' the Lord for!"

It seemed that nothing was going to prevent Papa from sending them back to town. Mattie packed what few clothes they had brought and presented them with their own freshly laundered traveling clothes. Cookie packed a basket for the ride and Patrick swept out the inside of the carriage.

"I don't want to go," Patsy whispered to Thomas and Caroline at breakfast.

"I don't either," Caroline said. "I miss Mama and Papa, but there are things we need to do here!"

Thomas excused himself from the table. He at least wanted to say good-bye to his home before he had to leave it—again.

He went through the mansion once, stopping to stare for a minute at the slash through Grandfather Daniel's face. He was headed toward the kitchen when he remembered something.

The bridge. He had to see the bridge one more time.

It was already muggy on the river, and Thomas felt like he was walking through a pillow as he made his way to the cove.

It's cooler in Williamsburg, he thought. *But I like it this way. I don't want to go back now!*

At least Dawson Chorley hadn't had a chance to tear the bridge down yet, and Thomas stepped onto it as if he were stepping into Bruton Parish Church. He leaned over the rickety railing and watched his face ripple up at him.

See? he thought. *I don't look that much different from the last time I saw myself in this water. Patrick and Mattie, they just forget—*

But as he stared at himself, another face took shape in the water, from the riverbank.

"No One!" he said softly.

No One smiled at him from where he squatted amid the brush and put his finger to his lips.

Thomas hurried off the bridge and joined the slave boy in his tiny hiding place.

"What are you doing here?" Thomas whispered. "You don't want another whipping."

No One tipped his chin up. "Won't nobody be givin' me no more whippin's," he said proudly.

Thomas's eyes went immediately to the slave boy's neck. "Where's your collar?" he asked.

"Don't need it where I'm goin'."

"Are you running away?" Thomas's palms turned suddenly sweaty like the rest of him. "Where will you go?"

"I'm goin' to join the army!" No One said. He smiled so big that Thomas was sure the corners of his mouth would slip off the edges of his face.

"But the Patriots won't take you if they find out you're owned by someone!" Thomas said. "Malcolm told me that."

But the boy was shaking his head happily. "I'm goin' with the men in the red coats. They come to Massa Ludwell's place and tol' me if I come and join them, they'd take care o' me."

Thomas felt his mouth fall open. "You're going to fight for the *British?*" he said.

No One nodded again. The ducking head and the terrified white eyes were both gone. The determined look of a proud almost-soldier had taken their place.

I don't guess it matters which side, Thomas thought, *as long as he gets away from here.*

Thomas nodded. "I'm glad for you, then," he said. "But maybe we'll see each other again sometime—when you're free."

No One bobbed his head, and Thomas stuck out his hand. The smile faded, and No One looked at it shyly.

"Shake," Thomas said. "We're friends . . . equals."

Slowly, the slave boy slid his palm against Thomas's. Thomas was about to give it a squeeze when he heard a voice from the riverbank above them.

"Thomas!" the voice said in a hoarse whisper.

No One jerked his hand away, and Thomas stood up.

"Patrick?" he whispered back.

"Yes!"

"I'm down here. Come on!"

Patrick slid down the bank on the seat of his pants and wiped them with his hands as he looked around. "Who were you talking to?"

Thomas looked around, too. No One was gone.

"No One," he said. "Did they send you to find me?"

"Yes."

"I'm not ready to go yet. Can you tell them you couldn't find me anywhere? I know that's a lie, but it's just a little one. I could owe you—"

Patrick was waving his hand in front of his face, and Thomas stopped.

"You don't have to leave," Patrick said. "You're staying here! Your father got a letter from someone by special messenger this morning, and he wants to read it to you and your mother and Malcolm. But I heard him tell your Mama, 'It looks like you all won't be leaving after all—not after this news.'"

Thomas hardly let him finish before he tore up the riverbank toward the house.

"Thank you!" Thomas called out as he ran.

"You're welcome!" Patrick called back.

Thomas didn't bother to tell him he hadn't been thanking him. He'd been thanking God.

The library was buzzing with excitement. Mama and Malcolm were already there, gathered around the desk, and Patsy and Caroline were sitting in a corner, eyes big as chargers.

"Sit down, Thomas," Papa said. "I want you all to hear this together."

Thomas's excitement fizzled. His father's face was grave, as if the news he had to tell them was bad.

Papa spread out a piece of weathered-looking paper on his desk and looked it over before he began to read.

> *Dear Father,*
> *I have no way of knowing whether you will receive this, but I must try to get word to you. I have been informed by—*

Papa mumbled and shifted his eyes a little farther down the page. He continued.

> *There has been fighting very near Williamsburg at a place called Spencer's Ordinary. We have scored a victory, Father—but the British left all of their wounded at the Ordinary and are headed for Williamsburg.*
> *I know you are on the plantation, and I beg you to stay there. Get Esther and Otis and any others you care about in town there, too, if you can. These men are not like the ones ravaging the plantations for*

supplies and sport. They have been dashing around the countryside chasing Lafayette for months, and they are nearly out of their minds with being battle weary. There is no way to tell what they might stoop to in a town with women and children and learned men like yourself. What's more, there will be trouble if Lafayette catches up to them. There could be a battle right at your front door. I promise you, I have this information on the best authority. I beg you to protect Mother and Thomas and the others.

    Yours faithfully,
    Samuel Hutchinson

"Who told him all that, John?" Mama asked. "Can this person be trusted?"

Papa rolled the paper quickly and glanced over to the corner where Caroline and Patsy were looking small and out of place.

"Ladies," he said, "would you go and tell Mattie that we would like some citron water?"

They nodded and left. When the door closed, Papa folded his hands on top of his desk.

"It comes from Alexander Taylor."

"But John," Mama said, "we don't really know which side Alexander is on!"

"We do now," Papa said quietly. "Samuel is certain of Alexander's loyalties."

"How did Alexander know you were on the plantation? He must be somewhere close by!"

Papa examined his quill pen. "He's a Patriot spy, Virginia. He's probably learned almost to be in several places at once.

He's a terribly bright young man."

Mama nodded and was quiet. Beside Thomas, Malcolm was so stiff that Thomas was certain he'd break. Papa seemed to sense it, too.

"Malcolm, I have no choice but to keep you here. You understand that, don't you?"

Malcolm nodded the way a stick would nod. Thomas couldn't stand it.

"But Papa!" he blurted out. "What about Patsy?"

"I was coming to that," Papa said patiently. "What would you say, Malcolm, if I were to invite Lydia Clark to join us here? She will need protection, too, and she has no one to take care of her. Patsy could get on with her service to Lydia while they're here. What say you to that idea?"

Malcolm didn't have to say anything. His shoulders relaxed, and he breathed from his very toes.

But Thomas stared down at his knees. His thoughts were tangled again. He wanted so much to stay here. He hadn't been able to think about anything else. But what about Caroline?

Papa stood up. "We must set out right away. Malcolm, I want you to go with me and bring Otis and Esther back. We'll take Patsy, in case Mistress Clark has made some other arrangements. And Caroline will go with us, of course—"

"But won't it be dangerous for her in Williamsburg?" Thomas burst out.

Papa cocked an eyebrow. "You forget, Thomas. Caroline's father is a Loyalist. I doubt the Taylors will come to any harm from the British. And the Patriots know now that they need Robert Taylor, what with his running the mill."

He looked at Thomas. "I have no right to keep Caroline here, son. A father must be allowed to make his own decisions for his children." He nodded Malcolm out of the room and picked up his quill pen. "Now if you'll excuse me, I have some business to attend to before we leave."

Thomas shook his head, which by now felt like a bowl of porridge. "You're going, too, Papa?" he said.

His father sighed. "Of *course*, Thomas," he said, clearly teetering on the edge of his patience. "If Williamsburg is to be invaded, I have preparations to make there, too. I will return as soon as I'm able."

He nodded toward the door again, and Thomas trudged from the room and out into the entrance hall. Servants were scurrying back and forth, carrying traveling bags and picnic baskets and chattering excitedly to each other.

"I can't tell you what it means to me to have Mistress Virginia back here to stay," Mattie said to a servant girl as they hurried through together.

Thomas sagged against the wall. *To stay? Is Papa really keeping us here for good?*

He felt as if his mind had been turned upside down and jiggled until everything in it was in a jumbled pile.

If that were true, wasn't that what he'd been wishing for and praying for? Wasn't this what he'd wanted—to be back in a place where he could run free all day and not have to go to work in the apothecary shop? And wasn't it better than ever without Clayton here to give him his lessons every day—and with Malcolm and perhaps even Patsy to have adventures with?

He slumped over to his spot under the stairs and sat down to hug his knees. *Maybe so*, he thought. But all he could really think about was Caroline. What was she going to do now? She'd have no one—not even her brother anymore.

Thomas felt a pang as he thought of Alexander. *Papa doesn't want Caroline to hear about his being a spy for us or he wouldn't have sent her out of the room. I surely don't want to be the one to tell her.*

"Thomas!" someone whispered.

Thomas jumped as Caroline peeked under and joined him with a tray full of glasses.

"I brought the citron water your Papa asked for," she said. She set the tray down and sat on the floor beside him, her flowered skirts billowing out around her.

She's already dressed for the journey, Thomas thought. A wave, just like the one he'd felt at the harbor, swept over him. *I'm right here at home,* he thought, *but I'm homesick.*

"He really didn't want citron water at all, did he?" she said, watching Thomas's face closely.

Thomas shook his head.

She sighed. "I suppose there's no talking him out of taking me home, is there?"

"No. I tried. He said your father has to make the decisions for you."

Caroline grabbed two handfuls of her dress. "I can't wait until I'm grown up. Then I can make my *own* decisions!"

"What would you decide then?" Thomas asked.

"To stay here and play at the bridge and prove that Old Red Eyes isn't fit to speak to your servants."

Thomas gnawed at his lip. "I'm not sure I want to stay here now."

"But you have to, Tom!" Caroline said. "You have to watch Dawson Chorley like a hawk and make sure he doesn't hurt Patrick or Mattie or anyone."

"How am I supposed to do that?" Thomas said miserably.

"You'll have Malcolm and Patsy to help you, of course, but you could do it alone. You're like a prince around here, you know. Next to your father, they respect you the most."

Thomas stared at her as she selected a glass of citron water and sipped at it.

"Me?" he said.

"Yes," she said, looking at him round-eyed. "You're a Hutchinson, just like those men in the paintings. You have the eyes. Sam and Clayton don't even have those."

She plunked the empty glass back on the tray. "I'd do anything to stay here and help you, Tom. I can hardly stand it that you and Malcolm and Patsy are going to have all the fun."

She looked almost shyly at Thomas. "You won't forget all about me and let Patrick or someone else take my place in the Fearsome Foursome, will you, Tom?" she said.

"No!" Thomas cried. "I would never do that!"

"Thomas!" Mama's voice rang out from the front door. "It's time for them to leave."

"Promise?" Caroline said.

He couldn't answer. He just nodded.

And he didn't have anything to say as he, Mama, Mattie, and Patrick stood on the front steps and waved until the carriage was out of sight at the end of the road.

He was just too homesick to talk.

⁜ ⚬⚜⚬ ⁜

Chapter Nine

*A*s that afternoon wore on through the heat like an old dog dragging its tail, Thomas felt lonelier than he ever had.

Mama helped Mattie and the servant girls clean up the dining room. Patrick was out in the stable working. Even No One was gone now, and Thomas didn't have the heart to go down to the bridge.

As the heat rose to its afternoon boiling point, he was about to head for the kitchen and see what Cookie had in the pantry when Patrick emerged from the stable. He was leading a black stallion Thomas had never seen before.

That must be one of the horses Dawson Chorley bought from the Fitzhughs this morning, Thomas thought.

He had taken only a few steps in Patrick's direction when Dawson Chorley was suddenly there, out of nowhere. He was already shouting at him.

"Have you got that horse groomed, boy?" he hollered.

Patrick's freckles stood at attention as he nodded.

"I beg to differ with you, boy! I can see from here that horse is no more groomed than I am!"

Mr. Chorley marched toward Patrick with a stride so hard that the dust came out in startled bursts under his boots. Thomas could see Patrick's Adam's apple bobbing nervously, and he knew his freckled friend was about to get a chewing out.

Thomas tucked himself behind the chicken house. He hated for anyone to watch *him* get yelled at.

But after a minute of Dawson Chorley's tirade, Thomas knew he'd never been talked to the way Patrick was being scolded . . . not even by Francis Pickering, who had given Thomas some pretty lengthy lectures. This wasn't scolding, it was screaming—complete with names for Patrick that Thomas had never even heard of. With his hands planted firmly over his ears, he slipped out from behind the chicken house and up the hill to the house. By the time he got to the back steps, his backbone was burning with anger.

And there wasn't a soul he could tell.

Mattie came out the back door just then, and Thomas said to her, "Do you know where my mother is, please?"

Mattie still stared at him every time he spoke to her. Finally, she said, "The last time I saw her she was in your father's library, Master Thomas."

"Thank you," he said.

But the library was empty when he got there. The maid had closed the shutters against the sun, and it was dark and cool. Sighing, Thomas shut the door behind him and crossed to his father's desk and sat in his chair. It was comforting there, even without Papa. It still smelled like him—licorice, horse soap, sweat, and lavender water.

The desk was orderly and polished, and Thomas reached out to run his hand along the bindings of the books that were stacked neatly near the ink stand. He knew those were his father's journals, where almost every night he recorded all the things that happened on the plantation.

That's who Papa talks to, Thomas thought. *His journals and God.*

Thomas picked up the quill pen and ran its feather along his face.

I hope when I'm grown I'll always know what to do and where to go, like Papa does.

He knew Caroline would have said, "You're a Hutchinson. You do know what to do!"

He let that roll over in his head several times before he slid open a desk drawer and found a piece of blank paper. Paper was scarce, but he'd write small and make it last. Dipping the pen into the inkwell, he began to write.

He started with the day Dawson Chorley had chased the Fearsome Foursome away from the horses, and he also wrote about the night the overseer had slapped Mattie and about Patrick's report that Dawson had been on his way to give him a whipping when they'd gotten word that the British were coming. Finally, he wrote:

And just this p.m., I heard him giving Patrick such a scolding in the stable yard it would burn a person's ears. Papa would never talk like that to anyone—

"Who is in here?" said a voice from the door.

Thomas let the ink drip from the pen as he looked up to see Dawson Chorley darkening the doorway with his hulking frame. His tree-bark fists were balled up until he saw Thomas at the desk and then his face startled into a smile.

I haven't done anything wrong, Thomas told himself firmly. *I'm allowed to be here.*

"I'm sorry, Master Thomas," Chorley said. "I wasn't told that you'd been instructed to do any paperwork."

I wasn't instructed to do anything, Thomas thought. But he didn't say it. He just nodded toward the door, the way Papa always did when he was ready for someone to leave.

"May I ask what your business is?" the big man said. "As overseer of the plantation, I like to inform myself about everything that takes place here."

He took a step closer to the desk, and Thomas quickly folded his paper. He looked up at Mr. Chorley and said, "It's private."

"Oh." A flicker of amusement went across the molasses-keg face, and Thomas felt annoyed. "If I can be of any help—"

"I'm fine," said Thomas. He wriggled in the chair and added for good measure, "That will be all."

Chorley didn't look quite as amused this time. He shifted his shoulders, nodded with a stiff smile, and left. When he was gone, Thomas breathed out a huge puff of air and tucked his paper under the stack of journals.

It must be nice to be Papa, he thought. *Then people know when to get away from you!*

The rest of that day droned on, and then the next. By the third day with no sign of Malcolm and the others, and no word of them either, Thomas thought he would crawl out of his skin. With Patrick too busy working to even talk, the only thing he could find to do was write in his journal. And even that he did only when he knew Dawson Chorley was far out in the fields.

But that still left hours with nothing to do . . . except chew on the nagging thoughts that were constantly in his mind.

Is Alexander really close by? And what about Sam? He must be, too, if he can get a message to us so quickly. Why don't we get a message from Papa? Is he all right? And Malcolm and Patsy? And Caroline? And then the sick wave would come over him.

By the time the fourth day began its slow crawl, he couldn't bear it anymore. He told Mama he was going for a walk.

"Don't go too far in this heat," she told him. And then she patted his arm and went back to her sewing. Thomas knew her thoughts were in their own tangle.

It was coolest in the deep shade of the woods, and Thomas cut through its lush greenness, heading away from the river. The woods hummed with hidden activity—the peepers, bees, and locusts—and Thomas felt a little less alone. He was humming along with them when he came out of the woods and found himself at the top of a grassy hill. Tendrils of smoke rising into the air and the smell of salt pork cooking told him he really wasn't alone at all.

Wiping the sweat from his forehead with his sleeve, he looked down, and his eyes sprang open. Right below him was a military camp, dotted with blue waistcoats and buff-colored breeches.

"It's the Virginia militia!" Thomas said out loud.

Papa had said they'd practically taken over Yorktown since the war started five years before, but until now Thomas had never really seen them. From up here, it was like looking at a picture of them in a book.

There were rows of white, triangular tents. At one end of the camp stood a big contraption over a fire pit with pots and kettles hanging from it. A few men stirred the pots, and others walked away with plates in their hands, looking none too excited about the contents.

I wonder if that's the way Sam lives now, Thomas thought.

And then it occurred to him that maybe someone there would know Sam. He headed down the hill.

The men at the cook fire looked too busy to talk, so Thomas walked along the first row of tents until he found one where several soldiers were gathered with their tin mugs and dented plates. A shriveled man with a face full of whiskers looked up at him.

"If you've come to join up, I think you're a mite too young," he said, and then slapped his knee and laughed at himself until he started to wheeze.

"Steady there, Whiskers," said a younger soldier with a front tooth missing. "You'll laugh yourself to death one of these days."

"I haven't come to join up—" Thomas started to say.

"Then it's dinner you want!" Whiskers cried. He patted the ground next to him. "You're welcome to join me!"

Thomas looked doubtfully at the watery soup in the mug. He would have mistaken it for dishwater if the soldier hadn't taken a gulp before he held it out to Thomas.

"I'm not really hungry either," Thomas said. "I just—"

"Then come set a spell!" Whiskers said, and waved him over.

Toothless rolled his eyes at a pudgy young man who was squatted next to him. "Don't sit down unless you have the rest of the day to spare," he told Thomas.

Thomas shrugged and said, "I do."

Toothless and Pudgy shrugged, too, and went back to cleaning their muskets. Thomas sat down beside Whiskers, who offered him a cold, misshapen biscuit. Thomas shook his head, and the soldier chomped into it with a loud crack.

"Hardtack," he said. "Ain't nothin' but flour and water."

Thomas nodded. This man would probably give his boots for one of *Esther's* sugar muffins.

"But at least we got water here," Whiskers said. "I got tired of drinkin' out of puddles in our last camp."

Finished with his feast, he wiped his hands on the dingy red lapels of his blue uniform waistcoat and pulled out a worn piece of paper from inside it. He reached toward the dismal little fire that was warming water near the opening of the tent and picked up a charred piece of wood. Thomas watched in amazement as Whiskers started to sketch on the paper with it.

For a while it was quiet, with only the sounds of a blacksmith hammering and a drummer practicing in the background. Whiskers worked his charcoal across the page and then looked up at Thomas.

"So what is your business here, if you don't mind my asking?"

"I'm looking for my brother," Thomas said.

"What's his name?"

"Sam—Samuel—Hutchinson."

The soldier paused and scratched at his whiskers for a minute.

"Infernal ticks," he said.

"Do you know him?" Thomas asked eagerly.

"Nope," said Whiskers. "But he must be a lucky man."

"Why?"

"Because he ain't here!"

Whiskers wheezed out another endless laugh, and Thomas tried to smile and not look too disappointed. After all, he hadn't really expected Sam to be here. In his letters he'd hinted that he was with the professional army, not the militia. Thomas looked around at the shabby camp.

If Sam were here, he'd liven this place up! he thought.

"So tell me about your games," Whiskers said.

Thomas's attention wandered its way back. "Games?"

"I'm of a mind to hear about young boys having fun, playing games," Whiskers said, still scratching away at his paper. "I'm too much surrounded by war and work."

It was surely better than wandering around the homestead, missing everyone. He wanted to tell about his friends and the things they all did.

"There's a bridge that my friend Patrick and I built a while back," Thomas said slowly. "It's in a hidden cove on our plantation. We'd hoped to have some games there."

"I'm sorry for you, boy," Whiskers said. "This war has turned all our lives upside down. But don't you worry. It'll be over soon."

"It will?" Thomas said.

"Sure. And the tide is about to turn in our favor."

"How do you know?"

"Well, from our spies, of course. We have some good ones now."

Thomas felt his ears perk up. "Do you know any spies?"

Whiskers closed his eyes and nodded sagely. "There's one in particular—smart as a whip he is." He stopped drawing and leaned forward. "He pretends to be a Loyalist and goes into the British camps and brings back information. He's a master, that one. A lot of folks still aren't sure which side he's on."

"Whiskers," Toothless said sharply. "Shut up."

"Oh, go on with you," he said, waving him off with his charcoal. "He's a boy. Who's he going to tell? Besides, he's on our side, aren't you?"

Thomas nodded firmly. "My whole family are Patriots, through and through."

"I knew that," said Whiskers. "That's why I done this likeness of you with our flag for a background."

He turned the piece of paper around, and Thomas felt his face break open into a grin.

"It's me!" he said. And it was, unmistakably. "How do you do that?"

"Gift from God," he said matter-of-factly. Then he glanced over his shoulder to where the other two soldiers had turned their backs.

"They'd have me strung up if they knew I done this," he said in a secretive voice. "But I keep it because it's one of my best."

He reached inside his waistcoat again and pulled out another piece of paper, this one dirty at the folds from being looked at again and again. "This is our spy," he whispered.

He carefully unfolded the paper. Thomas had to put his hand over his mouth to keep from gasping out loud.

There in front of him was a portrait of Alexander Taylor.

⁑ ⚜ ⁑

Chapter Ten

homas was sure the whole camp could hear his heart pounding as he watched Whiskers fold the portrait again and tuck it into his waistcoat. He wasn't sure how he managed to say good-bye.

"God go with you, boy," Whiskers said as he left. "I hope you find your brother."

I almost have, Thomas wanted to cry out as he tore up the hill and through the darkening woods. *I've found the next best thing, and he'll know where Sam is.*

He was sure he'd never run that fast as he flew between the trees and came out on the plantation side of the woods. His linen shirt was soaked through to the skin and his hair was plastered down on his forehead, but he didn't notice any of that as he raced toward the house.

But he stopped sharply when he came in sight of the stable—so sharply that he stumbled and sailed across the grass for several feet. Patrick looked up from where he was leading Burgess and said cheerfully, "Big, clumsy oaf."

"Is that Burgess?" Thomas cried. "Are they back?"

And then without waiting for an answer, he tore toward the house. Malcolm appeared at the back door.

"You'd better let me prepare you," he said.

"Prepare me for what, Malcolm?"

Thomas tried to give him a shove. Malcolm playfully shoved him back and planted himself in the doorway. "Are you ready for Otis and Esther?" he said. "Esther's been savin' up a lot of bossin' for you."

"I don't care!" Thomas cried. "Did you bring Patsy?"

"I did. And Lydia Clark, too."

"Is Papa all right?"

"He is now."

"Now? What happened?"

"He had a little tangle with the British is all."

Thomas craned his neck to see around Malcolm. "Did he come back with you? I want to go in, Malcolm!"

"He didn't come back with me, no, but he'll be along as soon as the British officers have moved out of your house in Williamsburg. You don't think he's going to leave them there alone, do you?"

"Our *house?*" Thomas nearly screamed. "We have British officers in our *house?*"

"They picked only the wealthiest homes, naturally. Yours, Mr. Wetherburn's, Robert *Taylor's—*"

"Robert Taylor's! Is Caroline—? Was she hurt?"

"Go inside and ask her yourself."

He stepped aside, and Thomas flung open the back door and slid into the hall.

"That must be Tom!" said a voice from the drawing room.

"Caroline?"

She poked her blonde head out into the hall and smiled. "I'm back!" she said. "And I've brought Mama with me!"

"*Your* mama?" Thomas said.

"Well, I don't know who else's mother I would bring. She's already in love with the homestead."

"But why is she here?" Thomas said.

Caroline's face clouded. "Oh, Tom, it isn't safe for anyone in Williamsburg now since the British have taken over—"

"Have they taken over the whole town?"

"They're all over the place—in the Courthouse and the old Capitol and most of the taverns, especially Wetherburn's. Mistress Wetherburn was so overwrought that Dr. Quincy had to give her some special medicine before he left for Spencer's Ordinary."

"Dr. Quincy went to the battle?"

"He went to take care of the soldiers. Even though they were British, he told Mama he thought they deserved to be cared for. Though I don't know what he was going to use to doctor them, what with the British taking all of Francis Pickering's supplies—"

"Why didn't he hide them like he's done before?"

"He was trying—and I was helping him—when the British soldiers came in and took it all, every last jar and bottle."

"You were *there?*" Thomas cried.

"Yes," Caroline said. "I was helping Francis since you weren't there to do it. They weren't even as polite as the ones who came here, Tom." She wrinkled her nose. "And they smelled bad. When they moved into our house, they made the whole place smell that way. Of course, that wasn't the reason Papa asked your father if Mama and I could please come here and stay. Papa was afraid to have them in the same house with us, even though he's a Loyalist." She took a deep breath and grinned. "Papa has moved in with Francis Pickering until they've gone, and here I am!" She leaned in close and whispered, "Do you have any more evidence to get rid of Old Red Eyes?"

At least that was a subject Thomas could make some sense of. He filled her in on what he had heard Mr. Chorley say to Patrick. Caroline listened, wide-eyed.

"Now that we're here to help you," she said when he was finished, "we'll have plenty to tell your papa when he comes back."

"Do you know when he's coming back?" Thomas asked.

"Soon, I think," she said. "That's what Malcolm says."

"What does Malcolm say?"

Thomas and Caroline looked up from their perch at the bottom of the stairs to see Malcolm coming toward them carrying a large trunk.

"That's ours," Caroline said brightly.

"How long are you two staying anyway?" Malcolm said, giving an exaggerated grunt as he hoisted the trunk. "I have to carry this upstairs. Come with me, and I'll tell you."

They followed him up to Caroline's room, where he wiped off his face with his shirtsleeve and caught his breath.

"It's Cornwallis himself who's in Williamsburg," Malcolm said. "He's living in the president's house at the college, and his men have made themselves at home with no thought for the townsfolk at all. They won't even let people draw water from their own wells." Malcolm's face darkened. "The streets are crowded with them, all swaggering about and clanking their swords. You wouldn't believe the flies they've brought in with their horses. Look at these bites on my arm."

"What's going to happen now?" Thomas asked.

Malcolm leaned on the trunk and smiled. "Lafayette, I think, will come to the rescue. He's been leading the chase all this time, and they say he's the one who drove Cornwallis into Williamsburg, where they can keep an eye on him while the Patriots gather more men."

"Who's staying in our house?" Thomas asked. "Do they smell?"

Malcolm chuckled. "Not since your father knocked one of them into the water barrel for talking bad talk in front of Esther. A bath was just what that officer needed—and he watched his mouth with John Hutchinson around!"

Just then, a harsh voice interrupted. "Did he now? Well, I think you'd better stop moving yours and get to work!"

Malcolm slid from the top of the trunk and stared at the doorway. Dawson Chorley filled the door frame with his huge arms. His sleeves were already shoved up past his elbows, and there was no politeness on his face, at least not for Malcolm.

"I beg your pardon, Master Thomas," he said, nodding vaguely, "and you, Mistress. But I understand your friend is no longer a guest of the Hutchinsons but is back to his duties as an indentured servant. That means that he works for me now."

Thomas felt as if the floor had just caved in and swallowed him up, and Caroline with him. Dawson Chorley closed his mean hand on Malcolm's shoulder and led him out of the room.

Caroline flew at Thomas. "Tom, no!" she cried. "He can't work for that awful man! You have to do something!"

"What can I do?" Thomas said. "Papa made him the boss of everyone on the plantation."

Caroline stabbed her hands savagely onto her hips. "Well, he's not the boss of me. He'd better not hurt Malcolm!"

"Caroline!" Betsy Taylor called from downstairs. "Where are you?"

"I'm coming, Mama!" she answered, and then she turned her round, brown eyes on Thomas.

"I hope your papa comes back soon," she said. "And when he does, if you don't tell him about Dawson Chorley, I'll tell him myself!"

With that, she flounced out of the room.

It was sunset by then, and there was nothing for Thomas to do but make tracks for the bridge. It was the only place where nothing else could go wrong.

The crickets were chirping in full chorus when he got there, and a group of bullfrogs had gotten together a quartet. No One would surely have seen the Lord in the sky, too. It was a glorious purple with trails of pink and orange that almost hurt his eyes. Thomas stretched out on his back and tried not to think about what Dawson Chorley was making Malcolm do.

God, he prayed suddenly, *I need another bridge—for Malcolm this time. Please.*

"Are you asleep there?" someone whispered.

Thomas opened his eyes and rolled over onto his side.

"No One?" he whispered back. "I thought you'd gone."

"No One?" said the voice. "No, I'm someone."

Thomas sat straight up and stared into the darkness. "Who's there?" he called softly.

"Here. Under the bridge."

Pins and needles prickled Thomas's backbone, and he crawled with painful slowness to the end of the bridge. He leaned over and peered underneath.

"Who are you?" he said.

"It's me, Thomas," the voice said. "Come see."

Thomas's heart stopped halfway up his throat. "Alexander!"

"*Shhh!* Quiet! Come down here!"

Thomas swung over the side of the bridge and sloshed to the bank, his heart hammering.

"I suppose you could make a little more noise, but I don't know how!" the voice whispered. "Quiet down, would you?"

Thomas knelt beside the bridge and stared into the darkness beneath it. He blinked furiously into the night. Slowly, a face emerged from the blackness and smiled a slice-of-watermelon smile. Brown eyes glowed in the last of the sunset's light.

"It *is* you!" Thomas whispered.

"Yes!" Alexander hissed back. "But don't say my name again. Just in case anybody is listening."

"They could be!" Thomas whispered fiercely. "We have a new overseer here who is *evil*."

Alexander put a hand on Thomas's arm. "I'm sure you and your little band will take care of that," he said softly. "But Thomas, you need to listen to me now."

Even in a whisper, Alexander's voice was urgent. It wasn't the playful, full-of-adventure voice that Thomas had come to love. He nodded solemnly.

"I talked to a friend of yours today—a soldier named Whiskers."

"I met him at the camp," Thomas said.

"I know. I talked to him for only two minutes before he was showing me your picture and telling me you liked to spend sunset at a makeshift bridge." Alexander paused and twinkled his eyes up at the bridge. "He wasn't fooling, was he?"

"I was just a boy when I built it."

"Never mind," Alexander said. He lowered his voice even more. "Whiskers means well, but he'll talk to anything that will stand still. There is no way to tell how many others he's told about me. But listen, Thomas, you must not tell anyone that you heard about me or that you've seen me. You can't tell your father or your friends." He stopped and looked straight into Thomas's eyes. "And especially not Caroline. If you do, she'll have to tell Papa, and it would give him so much pain. I am doing what I think is right, but I hope we can win the war without his ever having to know."

Thomas nodded. "I won't tell anyone. You have my word."

Alexander sighed and squeezed his arm. "That's something I know I can count on," he said. He motioned toward the bridge with his head. "Go on back to the house as if nothing happened."

But Thomas clung to Alexander's sleeve. "Will I see you again?" His voice was thick, and it was hard to swallow.

Alexander grinned. "Of course. When this war is over— and it will be soon—I have more to teach you than I ever dreamed was possible. That is, if you're willing."

Thomas grinned back and bobbed his head.

"Good, then," Alexander said. He pulled his arm gently away. "I'll count on that, too." He ducked down low under the bridge and was quiet.

Thomas stood there for a minute and then parted the tall grass. Alexander was gone.

I didn't have a chance to ask him about Sam, Thomas thought. Another sick wave washed over him.

✛ ✛ ✛

Chapter Eleven

"Well, a fine thing!"

Thomas opened a sleepy eye and groaned.

"I come all the way from Williamsburg, and you can't even come out into the kitchen and find me to say hello!"

"Hello, Esther," Thomas said. He tried to close his eyes again, but the old nurse already had the heavy drapes open.

"No!" he moaned sleepily. "Just a few more minutes, please!"

"Well," she said with a huff as she marched to the clothes press with an armful of shirts, "I can see you've grown used to being pampered again in a very short time."

"No, I haven't, Esther," Thomas said, burrowing his head.

"At least our Malcolm hasn't forgotten how to work. He was up before I was this morning, and he's already out—"

Thomas bolted up in bed. "What is he doing?"

Esther sniffed as she pulled another pile of clothes from the leather bag. "I'm sure I don't know. I thought he'd report to me for his duties, as usual, but I suppose they've got him doing—"

"Who's 'they'?" Thomas asked.

Esther steered her round body around so she could look at Thomas. "Whoever is runnin' this plantation now." She shook her gray head and clucked her tongue. "I'm sure I'll be glad when this war's over and we can get back to livin' like sane people."

Thomas hauled himself out of bed and stood in front of her in his nightshift. She looked him up and down and scowled.

"You've grown an inch," she said. "But you're thin as a fence rail. Aren't they feedin' you like I do?"

"No," Thomas said honestly. "But Esther, have you met the new overseer, Dawson Chorley?"

"No," Esther said. "He won't be overseein' *me*, nor Otis neither. Though I'm sure your father made that plain."

Thomas went to the window and looked out into the sunlight at the yard below. There was no sign of Malcolm, but Patsy was down there, holding Lydia Clark's hand and pointing in all directions. Thin, mousy Lydia looked a little bewildered, but then, she always did.

But at least she isn't a mean mistress, Thomas thought as he watched Patsy tug at her hand. He was beginning to appreciate people who *didn't* yell and hit and call people names. He turned to Esther.

"I can finish putting those away," he said. "I know where they belong."

Esther tucked in her chin. "You have something hidden in this clothes press you don't want me to see?" she said.

Thomas shook his head and took the pile of stockings she was holding. She looked at him for a moment longer and then left the room, muttering under her breath.

At breakfast on the morning porch, Mama was glowing as she poured the bee balm tea. On her left she had tiny Betsy Taylor with her pile of golden hair—enough for any two women, she often joked. And on her right was timid Lydia Clark, who was looking less timid by the minute as she nibbled on a pecan muffin. Patsy sat beside her mistress, and Caroline sat alongside her mother and let her squeeze her hand every few minutes.

Thomas felt like a second thumb in the midst of all those women and girls, and he wished someone who wasn't wearing ruffles would come and sit next to him.

"Now, Virginia," Betsy Taylor said, "I do not expect you to entertain me as if I were a guest here."

Mama looked scandalized. "Nonsense, Betsy!" she cried. "I am delighted to have all four of you, and I'm sure we shall have a lovely time. I refuse to let the war keep me from enjoying myself!"

Lydia laughed nervously. "You are a marvel."

"Still," Betsy said, "I insist that we do not disrupt your household. Caroline and I will work on our needlecraft. And this will be the perfect time to start on her sampler."

The other two women oohed and ahhed, and Thomas stole a glance at Caroline. She looked back and crossed her eyes, and Thomas had to smother a laugh.

"Your sampler!" Mama said. "I would be honored to be able to help, Caroline."

"Yes, ma'am," Caroline murmured.

"Does Patsy know about a young lady's sampler?" Mama asked.

Patsy shook her head.

"Oh, my. Well, it's a work of needlecraft that will have a place of honor on her sitting room wall when she's married."

Thomas nearly choked on his milk and had to bury his mouth in a napkin. Caroline glared at him.

"Perhaps Patsy should start one, too!" Mama cried. She put her hand on Lydia's arm. "I hope you don't think I'm stumbling in where I don't belong, but I don't have a daughter to teach all these things to." She grinned mischievously. "And Thomas has shown no interest whatsoever in needlecraft."

There was a chorus of female laughter, and Thomas scraped his chair back from the table, his face crimson.

"May I be excused, please?" he said.

No one answered. They were laughing too hard— Caroline loudest of all.

After breakfast, they gathered in the drawing room with their bolting cloth, thread, and their little needle cases to discuss what letters, numbers, verses, and designs would be stitched on. They would be there until dinner, they said, teaching Patsy and Caroline how to cross-stitch.

"And if they tire of that," Mama said as she closed the drawing room door, "we can knit. I have some wonderfully delicate bone needles, and wouldn't it be lovely to send the girls home with some tambour-worked pillow cases."

The door shut practically in Thomas's face. He scooted off toward the library to add to his journal, happy that he wasn't a girl.

But when he reached his father's library, the knob wouldn't turn. Thomas jerked it, but it wouldn't budge. He came out from under the staircase as Mattie was passing through.

"Mattie?" he said.

She looked up and stared her usual stare. And then she smiled softly.

"Yes, Master Thomas?" she said.

"Do you know why the library is locked?"

The smile faded. "Yes, sir, I do. Mr. Chorley ordered it."

"Mr. Chorley! What business does he have doing that?"

Mattie stepped back nervously. "I . . . he asked me if I knew where the key was and I told him and he locked it."

"But why?"

Mattie looked like she wanted to run. "I wish you wouldn't make me tell you, sir."

It was Thomas's turn to stare at her. "Make you?" he said. "I can't make you!"

"Can't you?" She looked truly surprised. "You're Master Hutchinson's son. You can order me to do anything you want . . . and you've been doing it all your life!"

Thomas didn't know what to say. She watched him for a moment and sighed. Glancing first over both shoulders, she moved her face close to Thomas's. "Mr. Chorley said he caught you going through your father's things, and he didn't think Master Hutchinson would like that."

Thomas felt anger sizzling up his backbone. Mattie saw it, and she nodded. "That's exactly how we all feel about him, Master Thomas. I don't know why Master Clayton ever hired him!"

"Did he hit you once?" Thomas asked.

Mattie put her hand up to her cheek and nodded.

"I'm going to tell my father as soon as he comes back," Thomas said fiercely. "But you'll have to come with me and tell what happened, all right?"

She thought for a minute and then nodded again. "I'll do it, Master Thomas—more for Patrick than for me. He picks on Patrick worse than anyone, though he seems to pay less attention to him now that he has Malcolm."

Thomas flinched. "Malcolm?"

"He was draggin' him out into the field before dawn this morning."

"He was dragging *Malcolm?*"

Mattie nodded.

"And Malcolm *went* with him?"

"He hadn't a prayer of doing otherwise, Master Thomas," Mattie said. "That big bull had him by the ear!"

Thomas grabbed his own ear. He'd been tweaked a few times by Esther, and it didn't feel good when she did it. He could only imagine how it would feel if Dawson Chorley . . .

And then Thomas dropped his hand. *Esther!* his thoughts shrieked at him. *She treats Malcolm like he's her own son. If she finds out Mr. Chorley is dragging her boy around by his body parts, she'll probably tweak his nose off!*

"Do you know where Esther is, Mattie?" he said.

Mattie rolled her eyes. "I saw her in the kitchen trying to tell Cookie how to make batter bread."

Esther was coming out of the kitchen building when Thomas got there. She was dusting off her hands as if she'd gotten Cookie straightened out and was now going on to put the next wayward servant in his or her place.

And I know just the one, Thomas thought.

Since there seemed to be no other victims in sight, Esther marched toward him with her ear-tweaking finger poised.

"What are you about this morning?" she said. "Everyone

else seems to have found something useful to do."

"I do have something useful to do," Thomas said. "But I need your help."

"This is not a time for ridiculous games, Thomas Hutchinson," she said. "There is a war going on and we—"

"It's about Malcolm."

Her mouth stopped, and she gave Thomas a hard look. "Talk to me, boy."

Within minutes, they were sitting on the steps to the servants' hall, and Esther was watching his face as if she could see the words coming out of his mouth. He started at the beginning and told everything he knew about Dawson Chorley. Through it all, Esther stared at his mouth and nodded. But when he got to the part about Malcolm, she narrowed her eyes and snatched up his arm in her gnarled hand.

"He took Malcolm out to the field by the ear?" she demanded.

"That's what Mattie told me."

"Well, that's a good girl, that one. She wouldn't lie."

Esther pursed her lips angrily, but to Thomas's surprise, she didn't leap from the steps and search out Dawson Chorley with a rolling pin in her hand.

"I wish the master were here," Esther said. "Though I'm surprised Mistress Virginia has done nothing about it."

"She doesn't know," Thomas said.

Esther's wrinkles came together in a frown. "Why haven't you told her?"

"What can she do?" Thomas said.

"Your mama may look like a piece of lace, Thomas Hutchinson, but since this war has started, she has taken matters into her own hands when she's had to. She'd take

this man to task in a minute if she knew an injustice was bein'
done." She cocked her old head. "Though I hate to put her
in that position now, what with her husband away and two of
her sons." She twisted her mouth and looked at Thomas.
"You think we can handle this on our own, do you?"

Thomas looked at her blankly. "We?"

"You and Malcolm and Otis and myself," she said. "As
soon as that mongrel lets him in from the fields, we'll put our
heads together and figure out somethin'." Her eyes blazed
inside their crinkled lids. "I'd like to go and give him a piece
of my mind right now, I would. But I don't think Malcolm
would like that. He needs to have some say in this."

She sat working her mouth for a time, while Thomas
could only gaze at her in amazement.

Is this the same Esther who raised me up? Thomas
thought. *The one who told me I was stubborn and selfish
almost every day? She thinks I can help her solve a problem?*

He looked up to find her watching him. "You meet us in
the kitchen after the supper things have been cleared away
this afternoon," she said. "And bring Patsy and that smart
little Caroline girl."

Thomas nodded.

"And you'd better bring Patrick along, too."

Again, Thomas just nodded. He was too surprised to say
a word.

At dinner, Thomas made a point to sit next to Caroline
at the table. While all the ladies were exclaiming over the
scalloped oysters, Thomas leaned in and whispered, "Can
you get away?"

Caroline shook her head and rolled her eyes. "We're

all to listen to Mistress Lydia play the harpsichord," she whispered back, "and then we have to take a *nap!*"

"Why?"

"Because that's what ladies do on a summer afternoon," she whispered in disgust. "Those three are having a wonderful time turning Patsy and me into proper gentlewomen!"

"Well, Thomas, you should be very proud of Patsy." Betsy flashed a teasing smile at Virginia Hutchinson. "She has true sewing fingers. She should have that sampler finished and be ready for a husband by Christmas!"

There were gales of laughter, and Thomas looked forlornly at his full plate. It was too soon to excuse himself from the table.

The time dragged by that afternoon, but at last supper was over and Thomas managed to coax Mama out of making Patsy and Caroline join the ladies for a board game in the dining room. Patrick was waiting for them outside the kitchen with word that only Esther, Otis, and Malcolm were inside.

"Esther told Cookie only *she* could cook Malcolm's dinner for him," Patrick said.

"Oh," Caroline said with a grin. "Poor Malcolm!"

But Malcolm didn't seem to care what was on his plate when they found him at the big table in the kitchen. Old Otis was whittling, soundless as always, by the fireplace, and Esther was sweeping dust that wasn't there off the hearth. Malcolm was pushing something brown around with his spoon. His face was as dark as the charred embers in the fire.

The children surrounded him, and Patsy sat closest. Malcolm just twitched an eyebrow and went back to the food he wasn't eating. There was silence in the kitchen.

Finally, Caroline poked Thomas.

"What?" he said.

"Do something, Tom!" she hissed at him.

Thomas looked at Malcolm helplessly. "Mattie told us he dragged you out to the fields today. I told Esther—"

Malcolm looked up at him darkly. "Why did you do that?"

Thomas stared. "I thought you would want her to know!"

"If I'd wanted her to know, I would have told her, lad," he said. "What good can she do? What can any of you do?"

Thomas looked at Caroline. She nodded him on.

"But all together we can surely do something," Thomas said. "We always have."

But Malcolm shook his head grimly. "You don't know what this man is really like. I do now—and this is no game, lad. I was wrong to ever suggest that it was. I tell you there's nothing to be done but wait until Master Hutchinson comes back. Until then, I can fight my own battles."

Caroline leaned across the table at him. "Malcolm," she said, "I think you're being pig-headed. Why don't you at least tell us what happened today, and maybe—"

Malcolm slammed his hands on the tabletop and shoved his way out of his chair. "I said no!" he shouted.

He stormed toward the door, and Patsy stood up on her chair.

"Malcolm?" she said.

He stopped with his back to her. "What, Patsy?" he said tightly.

"Where are you going?"

He closed his eyes. "For a walk."

"I want to go with you!"

"No."

"But I always go with you."

"Not this time."

"But Malcolm, I'm afraid."

He sighed, and for a moment Thomas thought he was going to say yes. Patsy must have thought so, too, because her face lit up, and she hurled herself at Malcolm's back for a ride, the way she always did.

Malcolm let out a scream that ripped through the room like a knife blade.

Patsy scrambled down and stood, white-faced, with her hands over her mouth. Malcolm doubled over and heaved until Thomas thought he would throw up right there on the floor. Then with a groan that seemed to come from the pit of his soul, he staggered out the kitchen door.

Esther started after him, but Otis stopped her with a grunt.

"He's hurt!" Esther cried.

"Let him be," Otis said flatly.

Esther snatched up the broom again and began savagely sweeping.

Caroline ran to Patsy.

"Tom?" she said. "What happened?"

"I think I know," Patrick said. His freckles stood out like thorns on his pale face. "I think he was beaten by Dawson Chorley."

✣ ✣ ✣

Chapter Twelve

sther clasped the broom to her as if it were Malcolm himself. "Otis, I cannot just let him be!"

Otis said something to her with his eyes, and she sank to a chair, still holding the broom.

"What do we do now, Tom?" Caroline said.

Run upstairs and pull the covers over our heads until Papa comes back! he wanted to cry.

He swallowed hard. And what would Papa do if he were here? Before he even went out to the field and dragged Dawson Chorley in by *his* ear, he would pray. Thomas knew that.

"We need a bridge," Thomas said.

Patrick looked at him with his mouth hanging open. "We have a bridge."

"No, not that kind. We need God to be a bridge."

Caroline stopped biting her nails. "Go on," she said.

"My papa says when there's nothing more we can do, we should pray for God to be the bridge between what's needed and what we can do."

"Then get a bridge for Malcolm, Thomas!" Patsy cried. She flapped her hands as if she didn't know where to put them without her brother there. "He needs one."

"Come here, little one," Esther said. Patsy ran to her, and Esther rocked her.

"All right, then, Tom," Caroline said. "Pray."

So Thomas prayed for a bridge and then he said "amen." They all opened their eyes and looked around as if they expected to see an actual bridge right there on the table.

"What do we do now?" Caroline asked.

"I'm not sure," Thomas said. "But I think we wait."

Esther bobbed her head in agreement. "And I for one am goin' to keep on a-prayin' for that bridge, and I'm goin' to tell Mattie and some of the others, too. You can never have too much prayer."

But for now, she kept rocking Patsy and stroking her hair.

Patrick left to do his nighttime chores, and Thomas and Caroline wandered back to the mansion together. It was the first time he had been alone with her since he'd seen Alexander, but Thomas wasn't worried about that now. That seemed so long ago that he wasn't even sure it was real anymore. Besides, she wouldn't be able to tell one worry on his face from another.

"I never hated anybody before, Tom," Caroline said. "But I think I hate Dawson Chorley."

"Papa says it's bad to hate."

"I know. I guess I'm just bad then."

Thomas looked at her. Her face was puckered and stiff, and there was no trace of her slice-of-melon smile.

"Tom?" she said. "I hope we find that bridge soon, because I don't like to hate."

It wasn't bridges that Thomas dreamed about that night as he tossed and turned inside his mosquito netting. It was Francis Pickering, scolding him for not delivering the soapwort and dovesdung plaster fast enough. He woke up sweating long after midnight and went to the window to open the heavy drapes. Esther always insisted on closing them, even in the heat of summer. She said the night air was bad for him.

How could this be bad? Thomas thought as he breathed it in—the salty smell of the York River, the scent of the honeysuckle growing up the side of the kitchen building, even the odors of the horses wafting over from the stable. They were all smells he loved.

Yet even as he sniffed them in, there was a little anxious feeling around his edges that hadn't been there before—not before Dawson Chorley had come.

I think I might hate him, too, he thought miserably. His stomach felt heavy, and he knew Caroline was right. He didn't like hating either.

May we have that bridge now, please, God? he prayed.

He was about to turn away from the window when movement below caught his eye. Someone was walking across the lawn. As Thomas watched, the figure stopped at the crest of the little hill that led down to the river and pulled up his nightshift, as if to let the air touch his skin.

No one else moved like that in the darkness, as sure-footed as if it were broad daylight. It was Malcolm.

Let him be, Otis had said in the kitchen.

Soapwort and dovesdung plaster, Hutchinson! Francis had said in his dream.

Thomas decided on Francis and hurried from his room and down the stairs. He knew Cookie kept some medicines in the kitchen building. He didn't find any dovesdung, but there was some soapwort that would help take away the sting.

Malcolm was still standing with his back to the river with his nightshift up when Thomas slipped from the kitchen and across the lawn. When he heard him coming, Malcolm yanked his shirt down and crossed his arms.

"It's all right," Thomas whispered. "It's just me."

"Go back to bed, Tireless," Malcolm said. He tried to make his voice sound stern, but he'd used Thomas's Fearsome Foursome nickname. That meant he wasn't mad.

"I have medicine for you," Thomas said hopefully.

"I don't need any—"

"Francis won't let me sleep unless I give it to you," Thomas said.

Malcolm's mouth twitched a little. "Can it put out a fire?"

Thomas nodded. Malcolm jerked his head toward the stable. "In there," he said.

The horses nickered sleepily and stomped around, but once Malcolm had settled into the hay on his stomach, they ignored them. Thomas spread some soapwort ointment in his hand and pulled up Malcolm's nightshift. Even in the dim light, he could see the Scottish boy's back, and he gasped.

The servant boy's skin was raised in angry red stripes as if someone had dragged a pitchfork across his back. Thomas had to hold his breath to keep from throwing up as he touched it gingerly with the ointment.

Malcolm moaned softly, and Thomas pulled his hand away.

"It's all right, lad," Malcolm said. "Nothing can hurt it any worse than it does already."

"How did he do it?" Thomas asked.

"Whip."

"Why?"

"He said I was an 'insolent cur' and an 'arrogant animal' and this was the only way I was going to learn my place."

"And you're not going to do anything?"

"Not until your father comes back at least."

Thomas rubbed on the rest of the medicine and sat back on his heels. Malcolm's breathing slowed as he lay there.

"Why won't you let us help you?" Thomas said.

"I can't even look you all in the eye, lad. How can I let you help me?"

"But why—?"

"Shame."

Thomas sighed. "I don't understand. If you didn't really do anything wrong, then how can he make you feel ashamed?"

"You've never been whipped, have you, lad?"

"No," Thomas said.

"Being beaten is humiliating, whether you deserved it or not. That's why he does it, so he can have power over everyone. He makes them think they have no power."

"I hate him!" Thomas said fiercely.

"Then he has power over you, too. As long as you hate him, you'll do things he wants you to do—like scream and throw fits—the way I guess you used to do when you lived here before. At least that's what they all tell me." Malcolm chuckled and then groaned.

"But I didn't hate anybody then," Thomas said.

"I think you did, lad. I think you hated *you*."

Thomas was going to have to think about that later. Now he looked at Malcolm's torn back and said, "You don't hate him?"

"I don't hate him. I hate what he does. That's what I want

to fight . . . but I can't. He's too powerful, lad. This is too much for the Fearsome Foursome or Fivesome or whatever we are now." He chuckled and groaned again. "I can never keep it straight, we seem to be takin' on new members so fast."

"Then we just have to keep him from hurting you any more until Papa gets here. And we have to be sure that Papa knows everything. I'm keeping a journal." He looked thoughtfully at Malcolm's back. "I hope this stays this way until he gets here so he can see."

"Thanks!"

"Oh, I didn't mean—"

"It's all right, lad." Malcolm sighed. "It feels better already. You can go on to bed. I think I'll sleep right here."

Thomas nodded, but his mind was far from bed. There was a plan taking shape in his mind, and he had to think it through before morning.

"Good night, Malcolm," he whispered.

But Malcolm was already asleep.

When the sun came up, Thomas was already making his rounds. Esther was first. She bobbed her head when Thomas told her what to do, and she said she'd pass Patsy's part on to her, since she was still asleep.

When Thomas told Otis what he wanted from him, the old man just grunted and nodded, and Thomas knew he could count on him.

Patrick wasn't quite as enthusiastic until Thomas told him he'd have a wooden whistle to use by breakfast time.

"But be careful," Thomas said. "We don't want you ending up with a beating."

Mattie was horrified when Thomas told her what had

happened to Malcolm, and she wanted to help, but she wasn't sure what she could do. When Thomas told her, she smiled a smile that was almost bigger than her tiny face.

"I'll do it, Master Thomas," she said. "I'll give you a signal when it's done."

By breakfast he had talked to everyone but Caroline. With all the ladies around, practically planning her wedding, it was impossible even to whisper anything in her ear. He decided he would have to take matters into his own hands.

"Mama," he said, while Mattie was serving the sweet mush. "May Caroline practice her knitting this morning by making a pen wipe for Mr. Chorley?"

Caroline choked and nearly spit tea all over the table.

"What a fine idea, Thomas!" Mama said. "He has so much paperwork to do with your father preoccupied in Williamsburg, I should think he could use a pen wipe."

Caroline shot musket balls at Thomas with her eyes, but he grinned and said, "Could she do it by lunch?"

"Of course!" Betsy chimed in. "What color should we make it, Caroline?"

"Black," Caroline said between her teeth.

As a discussion ensued about whether there was any black wool available, Caroline kicked Thomas sharply under the table.

"It's to help Malcolm," Thomas whispered, rubbing his shin.

"It had better be," she said.

When Mattie came in to gather up the breakfast things, she took Thomas's napkin and gave him another one, saying, "I thought you'd need a fresh one of these, Master Thomas."

Thomas smiled and put it in his lap. He unfolded it to reveal the key to the library door. Happily, he slipped it into his shoe.

When breakfast was over, Thomas hurried out to the kitchen. Esther was packing a basket with muffins and fruit, and Otis silently handed him a wooden whistle.

"I'd take this out to him myself," Esther said as she handed the basket to Thomas, "but I'm afraid I wouldn't be able to keep my mouth shut."

Otis grunted.

Thomas set out for the wheat fields with the basket over his arm. *Chorley's going to be too busy feasting and running here and there,* he thought. *He won't have time to beat anybody.*

There was Thomas's basket of goodies at 8:00, which Thomas insisted on sharing with him until 9:00. That was when Patsy appeared with a request from Mistress Hutchinson that he pick them some peaches and join them for a mid-morning snack. Thomas nodded to let her know she'd done just fine in making Mama think it was her idea.

Dawson Chorley was barely back by 10:30, and then a calf got loose and threatened to crash through the field if he didn't go after it. The servants, of course, couldn't stop their work long enough to handle that. As Mr. Chorley took off after the bleating baby cow, Patrick winked at Thomas, and Thomas knew he'd opened the gate, just as Thomas had asked him to.

By then it was nearly dinner time, and Caroline appeared with a dark-blue knitted pen wipe just for Mr. Chorley. He said he was most grateful, though he didn't look as if he really appreciated Caroline hanging about for as long as she did—until nearly 2:00.

"It's so interesting here in the fields," she told Mr. Chorley sweetly.

By then it was stifling hot, and Thomas let Patrick take over.

"Remember," Thomas whispered when Dawson left to get a drink of water, "if it looks like anything is going to happen, blow the whistle as hard as you can, and I'll come running."

"May I keep it?" Patrick asked.

"Just as long as there are no beatings," Thomas said.

And there were none—not while Thomas was in the library catching up on his journal and locking Dawson Chorley out. Not while Dawson was taking part in the special tea basket Esther sent out with Betsy and Lydia, who said they would be delighted when she asked them.

"I never saw him all day," Malcolm said late that night while Thomas was rubbing ointment on his back and Patsy, Caroline, and Patrick looked on.

"And you won't tomorrow either," Caroline said. "We have some wonderful ideas."

"I didn't get to blow my whistle," Patrick said.

Malcolm raised his head. "Good."

"And now," Caroline said, "we're one day closer to Mr. Hutchinson coming home."

"Hooray!" said Patsy.

"Do you know what, Tom?" Caroline said.

"What?"

"I think God gave us a bridge today!"

But Thomas didn't have an easy feeling. He was pretty sure this wasn't over yet.

✠ ⋅✠⋅ ✠

Chapter Thirteen

$\mathfrak{A}$ s it turned out, there was no need to keep Dawson away from the servants the next day. A thunderstorm rocked the night with its ominous thunder and jagged cuts of lightning. The rains came down in torrents that went on all day.

The servants busied themselves with inside jobs, and Mr. Chorley locked himself in Papa's library to do paperwork. Caroline begged her mother to let her and Patsy roll bandages for the soldiers instead of sewing. She set everything up in the sitting room and put Thomas to work, too. He scowled all morning.

"What are you pouting about, Tom?" Caroline said.

"He said *I* was going through Papa's things . . . and that's exactly what *he's* doing! I have more right to them than he does."

She propped up his hand and began to wrap cloth around it. "Do you think he's found your journal?" she asked.

"I don't care if he does," Thomas said sullenly. "I'm not

afraid of that cow anyway."

"Tom, you are such a liar," Caroline said. "Hold still."

"He's the liar! And I hate . . . what he does."

"But it's all right," Patsy said. She smiled her crooked-tooth smile. "We're one day closer to Mr. John Hutchinson coming back."

"What day *is* it?" Thomas asked.

"The fourth day of July," Caroline said.

Thomas counted on his fingers. "It's been five years since the Declaration of Independence." He scowled fiercely again. "Then why isn't everyone free yet?"

"Be *still*, Tom," Caroline said, "or some poor soldier will have a crooked bandage." She pulled the rolled piece of cloth from his hand and looked at it thoughtfully. "I hope Alexander never has to wear one of these, but if he did, wouldn't it be something if he got one of mine? Of course, these are going to the Patriots."

Thomas quickly picked up another piece of cloth and bound it around his hand with a vengeance. "Not so much talk, Caroline," he said. "And more work."

He'd promised Alexander, but he still felt guilty keeping a secret from his best friend.

By supper the rain had stopped, and it dripped lazily from the roof as the children gathered on the servants' porch with Esther, Otis, Malcolm, and Patrick, eating some leftover tarts Cookie had set out for them. She seemed bent on taking care of them while they continued their mission.

"There's somethin' so refreshin' about the world after a rain," Esther said.

Caroline selected a strawberry tart and nibbled it daintily. "The rain washes all the evil away."

Malcolm grunted. "Not for long. I see Old Red Eyes didn't get washed away."

He jutted his chin toward the stable, where Mr. Chorley was just going in. Patrick sat up uneasily on the porch railing.

"What's wrong, Patrick?" Caroline said.

"He's going to check on the way I hung up the harnesses."

Malcolm said, "No matter how well you did it, he'll find some fault with it. I've known common thieves kinder than he is."

"I think the devil himself is kinder than Dawson Chorley!" Thomas said.

Otis grunted as he whittled his piece of wood.

"What are you making tonight, Otis?" Patsy said. She curled up next to him and shined her enormous green eyes at him.

He held out his palm to her.

"What is it, Patsy?" Caroline said.

Patsy held up a little wooden figure. "It's a face!"

"Whose?"

A soft giggle slipped out of her, and she covered her mouth with her hand.

Malcolm took the figure from her and studied it. He let out a guffaw. "You're an artist, Otis! Look, it's Old Red Eyes!"

Thomas leaned in to look. Sure enough, it was a perfect likeness of Dawson Chorley with his ugly, rectangular slit of a mouth and his mean eyes with their iron-looking rings.

"If you could make it growl, it would be perfect!" Malcolm said.

"I can!" Thomas cried. He snatched the figure from Malcolm and held it up. "'All right ya plebeian herd! Every one of you start cutting that wheat with your teeth, or I shall have you baked in Cookie's batter bread dough!'"

Everyone howled, and Caroline clapped her hands. "Do some more, Tom!" she cried.

Thomas held the figure up again and was about to begin. But there was a heavy footfall on the steps behind him.

"I beg your pardon—"

Thomas thrust the figure inside his shirt and looked at Caroline. Her eyes were flashing, but she was sidling closer to Esther. Malcolm and Patrick both stared at the floor.

As if they've become different people! Thomas thought.

"Master Thomas, ladies, I must speak with this woman, if you'll excuse me?"

Thomas followed the overseer's gaze to Esther.

Esther turned her head sideways and looked at Dawson out of the corner of her eye. "Are you speaking of me?"

"I am. I have business with you, woman."

Esther drew herself up. "My name is Esther, and I'll thank you to call me that. As for these children, anything you have to say to me, there's no harm in them hearin'."

Mr. Chorley's face darkened like a thunderhead, and he glared at Thomas. But Thomas didn't move. He couldn't wait to see what Esther was going to do next.

"Very well, *Esther*," the man said in a tight voice. "I want to know what you mean by thinkin' you can sit here with the master's children when there's work to be done."

Esther came out of her chair and straight at the overseer until her nose nearly touched his chest. He couldn't have missed the blaze in her eyes. Behind her, Otis stood up.

"I was *born* on this plantation, mister," she said. "And not an evenin' has gone by that I did not pass the time with some member of this family." The loose skin on her wrinkled neck was trembling like a turkey's. "As for work to be done, Master Hutchinson never asked me to do a lick after—"

"Master Hutchinson is not here, you brazen old shrew. I have been put in charge, so you work for *me* now. My bed linens have not been changed since I arrived. See to them."

He started to turn away when a low growl came from the corner of the porch. Otis's face had hardened into a mask.

"If it's a job you want, old man," Dawson Chorley said, "you'll get none from me. You're useless around here, and it's time you were put out to pasture. I'll be speaking to the master about that when he returns—and you, too," he said to Esther, "if you don't start pulling your weight. Now get moving!"

"Esther," Otis said woodenly, "don't you go anywhere."

Esther folded her arms across her ample chest and sniffed. "I wasn't plannin' on movin' an inch," she said.

But Thomas could see her skirt trembling, and he heard the catch in her voice. Even she was frightened by this bull flaring his nostrils.

"I guess you're deaf, too, old man!" Dawson shouted. "I *said* she's working for me now, so why don't you just sit down there and pick what teeth you have left?" He flipped his face back to Esther. "Go, you old sow, before I get out the prod!"

This time Otis didn't say a word. He just lunged stiffly toward Mr. Chorley—with his whittling knife clutched in his hand.

"Otis, no!" Malcolm cried. "He'll take you down!"

He leapt across the porch at the old man and grabbed his arm, just as Otis was about to bring the little knife down across Chorley's shoulder. Otis stood like a tree while Malcolm pried the blade from his fingers. His old eyes were wet with the sting of anger.

"You're a viper!" he cried, his voice cracking. "You keep away from her!"

Dawson did turn from Esther—and took a menacing step toward Otis.

"Miserable old man . . ." he started to say.

But he never had the chance to finish. Malcolm pulled back his fist and drove it right into Mr. Chorley's belly. The air came out in a heaving gasp, and the overseer curled over. Malcolm hurled himself onto the man's back and held on.

"You can beat me until I'm dead!" he screamed in his ear. "But don't you touch him—or her either!"

By now, Caroline was wrapped around Thomas's arm at the end of the porch, and Patsy was plastered against his leg. Even Patrick had crept next to him, freckles standing out from his face. As the four of them watched in terror-stricken silence, Malcolm tightened his grip around the big man's neck. He held on for so long that Thomas thought Chorley was going to stumble from the porch.

You've beaten him down, Malcolm! Thomas wanted to cry out.

But Chorley gave a mighty shrug and Malcolm slid off his back. When the big man turned to look at Malcolm, his eyes were glassy with rage.

"Miserable mongrel dog!" he screamed. He reached out his hands, hard as tree bark, and clawed them into Malcolm's shoulders. Malcolm tried to wrench himself away, but Dawson Chorley picked him up and, with his teeth grinding, heaved Malcolm over the porch railing. Malcolm flopped to the ground like a rag doll and lay still.

Thomas felt a scream shudder through Patsy. She let go of his leg and went for the steps. Thomas and Caroline grabbed her by her skirts before Mr. Chorley could catch her with the toe he flung out in her direction.

"You stay away from him—all of you!" The hulking man's words spat out like yellow sputum. "I will do my job as I was instructed, and I will take no orders from anyone except Master Hutchinson himself! Now you stay away."

Esther was shaking. She pulled her quivering hand away from her mouth and shrieked at Chorley, "What are you goin' to do with him? He's hurt!"

"I'm locking him up. He'll get better soon enough."

Dawson Chorley gave them all one last glowering look before he took the steps, snatched Malcolm from the ground, and shoved him, staggering, toward the woodshed.

Esther crumpled into her chair. "He's hurt, Otis!" she cried.

Otis flexed his stiff old hands helplessly and put them on her shoulders. His face cracked.

Thomas watched over Patsy's sobbing head until Mr. Chorley gave his final push and sent Malcolm sprawling into the woodshed. Caroline tugged at his arm.

"We have to do something, Tom! We have to!"

Thomas clutched his head with both hands.

"I don't *know* what to do!" he cried.

"You tell your mama *now*, Thomas!" said Esther. She was hiccuping between words, but the fire was back in her eyes. "She's the head of the house with your papa gone."

Thomas nodded and gathered himself up from the floor.

He got to the door that led into the mansion and turned back to look at them. Five panicked faces looked back at him. It was as if Dawson Chorley had come in with a whip and lashed the courage out of every one of them.

And I'm going to go ask my mama *to stand up to him?* he thought as he closed the door behind him. *My mama, who knits and pours tea and turns the war into a chance to have a party?*

He crossed through the butler's pantry and into the drawing room, his head hanging nearly to his belly button.

Thomas stopped in the doorway. Mama was the only one there. She sat in a chair beside the window with her needlework on her lap, her head lolled against the red velvet. Her eyes were closed, and she breathed wearily, as if she had been too tired to climb the stairs and go to bed.

Mama can't be a bridge, can she, God? Thomas felt his throat get tight. *If only Papa would hurry back.*

He caught his breath as the next thought came to him.

Papa would *hurry home if I went to fetch him.*

Thomas took one last look at his mother, sleeping in the chair like a troubled little girl.

"I'll go get Papa for us, Mama," he whispered.

The night was black and the air as soggy as unbaked bread when Thomas crept out the back door a few hours later and scanned the yard with anxious eyes. Everything was still—not even the leaves were stirring. The storm had left the plantation silent and sleepy.

I hope Dawson Chorley is sleeping soundly, Thomas thought as he made his way to the stable, keeping in the shadows.

He was almost expecting to see Patrick there polishing the bridles when he opened the stable door. But there was no one except the horses, who didn't even whinny as he slipped into Burgess's stall and stroked the big bay's neck.

"I don't have time to saddle you up," Thomas whispered as he slipped a bridle over his head. "I hope you don't mind me riding bareback."

Burgess just tossed his mane drowsily and followed Thomas to the stable door.

"Walk softly," Thomas whispered. "Tiptoe if you can."

He knew he was talking more to keep from quivering into

141

a puddle than anything else. He'd never been sure of himself with the horses like Sam or Malcolm or even Patrick.

Thomas passed from the stable to the woods without making a sound. He led Burgess to a stump and stepped up on it and prepared to mount the horse. Suddenly, he heard a creaking sound.

Thomas tried to pull Burgess into the woods. But the sharp movement startled him, and the horse gave a high-pitched whinny and pulled away. Thomas froze.

Footsteps crunched across stones, and he knew someone was walking the path from the woodshed to the stable.

Once more, Thomas pulled on the reins, and still Burgess dug his hooves in and ducked his head. He heard an angry voice call out, "You there! Boy!"

Thomas had to force himself to look back. The bulky form of Dawson Chorley was outlined by the night. His face was directed toward the servants' porch. Again, he shouted, "You there! What's your name?"

"Patrick," a voice answered timidly.

"There's a horse missing, boy!" Mr. Chorley said roughly. "Do you know anything about it?"

Suddenly, Thomas knew he couldn't watch another one of his friends be hit, kicked, or whipped. He turned and gave Burgess a sharp slap on the rump. "Git!" he whispered to him.

Burgess took off like a shot toward the stables. Thomas waited only for the instant it took to hear Patrick cry, "There he is, sir!" Then Thomas turned and ran into the sheltering darkness of the trees.

He ran until he thought his side would tear out, and then he ran some more. The shadows whipped past in a blur and branches struck at his face, but he kept on until he was sure there was no one running behind him. Finally, he sagged against a tree and gasped for more breath. His thoughts were drumming madly, but they had a rhythm he could follow.

Head away from the river, they said. *Head for the road to Williamsburg.*

He'd made the trip only a few times in his life, and then it had been in a carriage pulled by four horses—not on foot in the black of night. But he knew the woods, and he found his way out to the road that connected with the Hutchinsons' drive. There would be no one there this late.

Thomas smeared at his lips with his sleeve and slowed to a walk. *If I keep to the trees, I can get past the drive, and then I can run along the road,* he told himself. *And I can't think about Chorley or I'll get off my path.*

By the time he reached the trees just beyond the place where the Hutchinsons' drive met the road, Thomas had to stop again and hug a tree to get his breath. It was 12 miles to Williamsburg. He knew he would never get there if he tried to run all the way.

I'll just run until I get past the drive, he coached himself. *And then I'll walk all the way till morning.*

He peered cautiously around the tree and strained to listen. The night was so still that he could have heard a leaf drop from a tree branch. Thomas took a step out and leapt to the next tree and waited again. The drive was only one more tree away. Then he could scamper across the drive and be on his way.

He made the leap without a sound. *Malcolm would be proud of me,* he thought. He almost smiled to himself as he held his breath and dashed across the driveway. He'd barely gotten to the middle when he heard trees crash and hoofbeats thundering toward him.

Biting back a yelp, Thomas dove for the trees on the other side of the drive and rolled to the ground. He planted himself behind a stump.

The hoofbeats slowed on the drive, and Thomas squeezed his eyes shut tight. *Please, God, please,* he prayed. *Please be my bridge!*

The horse stomped impatiently in the hard-packed dirt. Finally the rider clicked his tongue, and the horse trotted back toward the plantation. Thomas lay curled in a ball until the sound had long faded.

Then he got to his feet and ran, crouching, toward the road. He didn't stand straight up until he'd rounded two bends in the road. And then he ran as hard and as fast as his thundering legs would take him.

Thomas finally slowed to a walk when the marshes on either side of the road hardened to dry land and he knew the plantation was several miles behind him. His legs were hardening, too, and feeling almost too heavy to move.

He trudged on and tried to think about Patrick, cringing every time Dawson Chorley came near. And Mattie scurrying to stay out of his way. And Esther changing the linens on the cruel man's bed. And Malcolm locked in the woodshed.

We don't even treat our animals that way! Thomas thought. And he straightened his shoulders and walked on.

But after another mile, his eyelids began to droop, even as he walked. He shook his head and dragged his sleeve across his eyes. In the brush, something was startled and shook the bushes as it darted away under the cover of leaves. Thomas jumped and then slapped himself on both cheeks.

It was just a rabbit or something, he said to himself. *I'm starting to imagine things!*

But a minute later, he knew he didn't imagine the sound of horses' hooves and wagon wheels behind him. He looked around madly for a place to hide and only managed to flatten himself behind a large rock when the wagon rounded a curve and creaked and lumbered by.

Thomas peeked from over the rock, and he felt his eyes bulge.

The wagon was driven by a man in a dark-blue waistcoat and buff breeches. Beside him, a second soldier sat with his head nodding in sleep and bouncing with every bump in the road.

The militia! Thomas thought. *Where are they going this time of night?*

Surely not to Williamsburg. That shabby crew wouldn't walk right into the town where the British were settled.

Thomas cocked his head and listened. There was another wagon coming up the road behind them. If they weren't going to Williamsburg, they were at least going in that direction, and a little rest might make his legs strong enough to walk some more.

But I have to hurry or the soldiers in the next wagon will see me, he thought.

Slipping out from behind the rock, he kept low and hurried toward the side of the road. Just as the wagon went by him, he sprang up and grabbed the sides. His hands clung to the wood while his legs kicked him up, and he was able to scramble over the top and into the wagon bed.

He stifled an "ouch" as he landed on top of something hard. Whatever was in the wagon bottom was covered with blankets. Thomas lifted one and peeked underneath.

There must be 50 muskets here!

But there was still room enough for him. He pulled the blanket over his head and wriggled under it. Within minutes there was sweat running straight down his middle.

But it's better than walking, he decided.

And with the rocking of the wagon and the warmth of his makeshift bed, his eyelids grew heavy, and he closed them.

They couldn't have ridden much farther when he was jolted awake. His thoughts groped to make sense out of what was happening. The wagon had stopped. And men were shouting. And the blanket was being ripped off him.

"We got nothin' you want!" someone shouted.

"Indeed?" someone else said. "But I always wanted a boy 12 years old!"

I'm 11, Thomas thought in his daze.

Then his eyes sprang open, and he scrambled to get to the side of the wagon. A pair of strong hands caught him and yanked him backward. His head hit a musket on the floor of the wagon, and for a moment stars danced before his eyes.

"Where did he come from?"

"It's only a boy. Leave him alone!"

"Good heavens, it's our young Patriot!"

The last voice sounded familiar, and as Thomas felt himself being dragged over the side of the wagon, he pried his eyes open to see. A soldier was standing up on the seat of the wagon behind them, and his face was covered with whiskers.

"Don't you remember him?" Whiskers was saying.

"Shut up, old geezer," said another man. He turned to Thomas and barked, "And you put your hands up!"

Thomas's head was clear then, and as the man with the

strong hands dragged him to the side of the road, Thomas whipped his head around to look at the men who suddenly seemed to cover the countryside. They all wore scarlet coats and white breeches, and everyone had a shining sword swinging near his backside. He was right in the middle of the British army.

The British soldiers must have intercepted the wagon I climbed into, he thought wildly.

Thomas squirmed and got one arm away from the soldier's grasp. "Let me go!" he cried. "Leave me alone!"

Several of the soldiers laughed as the strong-handed soldier groped to get hold of him again.

"What are you doing?" someone else shouted. "Let him go. We haven't time for that! Unload these weapons!"

The soldier reluctantly loosened his grasp on Thomas, and he lunged forward. Suddenly, there was a foot in front of him, and Thomas tripped and tumbled end over end to the side of the road. There was a mild roar of laughter as Thomas clawed at the dirt to get upright again.

"Say, Dickinson!" said a voice above him. "Isn't that the boy—that young Hutchinson?"

"Well, Knox, for once I think you're right," said another.

Thomas felt a foot being planted in the middle of his back. Try as he might, he couldn't get up.

"I think the captain might have some use for him, don't you?" Dickinson said.

"I do! Hutchinson was the one who cheated us. I know it."

"Well, he won't cheat us out of his son. He should bring a fine ransom, eh?"

"You're fools, both of you!" another soldier shouted at them. "We aren't supposed to bother any women or children."

"This is no child!" Knox told him. "He almost sliced my arm off one night!"

The soldiers muttered and went back to gathering armfuls of rifles and muskets from the beds of the three militia wagons, while Dickinson ripped a length of cloth from the front of a Virginian's shirt and Knox yanked Thomas's hands behind his back and tied his wrists with it.

"Let me go!" Thomas screamed. "You can't hold me here!"

"They were all screamers, those Hutchinsons," Dickinson said as he bound another length of cloth around Thomas's ankles. "Shove one of those into his mouth."

The next time Thomas opened his mouth to scream, it was filled with a piece of rag he nearly gagged on. Knox picked him up roughly and hoisted him over the back of a horse.

"Let's take him to the captain," Dickinson said.

Facedown across a horse in front of wide, smelly Dickinson, Thomas could do nothing but hang like a boneless chicken.

I'll get to Papa all right, he thought as he swallowed hard so he wouldn't cry. *After he has to pay to get me back!* He tried not to think about what could happen to Malcolm by that time.

It seemed as if they had ridden for hours when the horse finally slowed and Dickinson wobbled his way to the ground. He was almost licking his chops as he slid Thomas off the horse and tried to heft him over his shoulder.

"He's heavy as a bag of bricks!" he said to Knox.

"So drag him," Knox said.

Dickinson shook his head. "The captain won't want damaged goods."

Thomas felt like "goods" as Dickinson squatted down to untie the cloth from around his ankles. He looked around miserably—and his eyes focused. He was standing in front of the Yorktown Courthouse. Right across the street was the Swan Tavern, where so long ago he'd sat with his family and friends and thought his biggest problem in the world was not seeing his plantation again.

I'd give the whole homestead just to get to Papa and save Malcolm, he thought as he blinked against the sting in his eyes. *Please, God, I need a bridge.*

With his ankles free, Thomas was able to hobble between Dickinson and Knox up the steps and inside the courthouse. Thomas could see that rows of benches had been ripped out, and the American flag lay in a heap in a corner on the floor.

There was a circle of men gathered around a table studying a map when Dickinson and Knox dragged him up to them. One held up a candle and scowled.

"What on earth? You two are idiots!"

But then another man turned around, and Thomas's heart sank even further. It was the captain who had ridden Papa's horse up the staircase of the mansion. He stared blankly at Thomas for a moment, and then his eyes took on their mad gleam.

"It's young Master Hutchinson!" he said. "Have you come to apologize for cheating us out of our bounty, sir?"

Several of the men looked up curiously from their map.

"What is this, Rippon?" said one of them. "Another of your game pieces?"

"Not this one," he said. "This one is not a game at all."

A shadow passed across his face as he came away from the map table.

"We thought you'd want to consider asking for a ransom—"

"Of course I do!" The captain sneered at Thomas. "And

I'm sure this time his father will be much more cooperative."

Thomas squirmed and tried to shake off his guards, but both of them only gripped his arms harder. The captain gave a harsh laugh.

"Rippon!" someone called from the table. "We must finish, or we shall have Lafayette on top of us before we have the other half of the men across the ford!"

The captain gave Thomas one last evil smile before he backed toward the map table. "Take him to my quarters. I shall write the ransom letter as soon as I've finished here."

Thomas writhed again and this time got a shoulder away from Knox. He tried to spit out his gag, but Knox had control of his arm again and Dickinson pushed the rag farther into his mouth before he could make another move.

"I'm glad to get rid of him," Knox muttered.

"Amen," Dickinson said.

They dragged him out of the courthouse and out into the street. Although it was still the wee hours of the morning, the road was teeming with red-coated soldiers who all seemed to be making ready for something.

Dickinson and Knox dragged him across the street, and Thomas's eyes popped as Knox kicked open the door of the Swan Tavern. He looked around wildly for Mr. Gibbons, but he was nowhere in sight. Neither were any of his servants—or the tables with their snowy-white tablecloths and trays steaming with seafood. Thomas looked sadly back at the dining room as they dragged him toward the stairs.

I'll never sit with my family like that again, he thought. *Perhaps I'll never even see them again!*

His feet banged against the steps, and Knox gave him an impatient shove.

"Watch where you're goin'!" he said.

"Here's what we'll do," said Dickinson. "When we get him to the captain's room, we'll make that black boy look after him."

Knox nodded like a pigeon. "Yes! You know, it's a pity we English don't believe in slavery."

"Indeed it is," said Dickinson. "That's the only thing I've been able to make sense of since I came here." They stopped outside a room on the second floor, and he nudged Thomas with his foot. "I cannot possibly believe that any good quality can exist in an American." With that, he knocked the door open with the same foot and shoved Thomas inside. "Now then, boy, I don't think you're smart enough to get away, but just in case you have any such ideas, let's put them right out of your head."

Gleefully, the soldier leaned over and ripped off Thomas's shirt, tearing it to shreds. Knox appeared to catch on and dragged down his britches, leaving Thomas in only his underdrawers.

"That should keep him off the streets, eh?" Dickinson cried.

He was still laughing and snorting as he slammed the door and faded off down the steps with Knox.

Thomas rested his cheek against the warm floorboard, and for a moment he was just glad to be rid of them. When the door opened again, he groaned silently.

But a black, shiny, cleanly shaven head poked its way in, and a pair of round, black eyes met his. Their whites began to shine as a smile broke over his coffee-colored face. He closed the door behind him and reached down and pulled the rag from Thomas's mouth.

The first words Thomas said were, "No One!"

✢ ✢ ✢

Chapter Fifteen

homas grinned, even before No One got the ties off his wrists.

"You did join the British army after all!" Thomas cried. "I wanted you to be a Patriot, but now I'm glad—"

No One glanced warily toward the door.

"I wasn't 'spose to take that gag out of your mouth," he said. "I was only 'spose to tie your ankles to the bed."

"You can't, No One!" Thomas whispered hoarsely. "You have to help me get away!"

The shimmer disappeared from No One's eyes. "Oh, no, sir. I can't do that."

Thomas's shoulders dropped. "You'll get in trouble, won't you?"

No One nodded. "But I can get you something to eat before I tie you up again."

"I don't want anything to eat," Thomas said miserably. "I just want to get out of here."

He stopped and looked at No One, who was casting

152

frightened glances toward the door.

"You're no more free than you ever were, are you?" he said.

There were footsteps in the hall, and No One snatched up the cloth and began to tie Thomas's wrists with it. The footsteps stopped outside the door, and No One grabbed for one of Thomas's ankles as the doorknob jiggled.

"Captain!" a voice called from farther down the hall.

"What is it?" said the captain outside the door. "I have a prisoner to attend to."

"Not now, you don't. The commander wants to speak to us about that spy. He's been about again."

The captain gave an irritated sniff. "What is there to talk about? If I see him, I'll shoot him."

"And you'll end up in the stocks for it! The commander wants him brought in alive."

The captain gave a grunt and moved away from the door. Thomas let out a long breath as he heard the footsteps going down the stairs.

By now, No One had his ankles strapped to the bedposts, and he stood looking sadly at the gag.

"Go ahead," Thomas said, "put it in."

No One gently pressed the gag into Thomas's mouth and then hung his head. Thomas tried to shrug to let him know it was all right.

It doesn't matter, he thought. *I'm not going to get to Papa anyway—and the hateful people are going to keep winning.*

He tried not to think that God hadn't provided a bridge.

The black soldier kept his eyes to the floor as he backed out of the room. The click of the latch was the loneliest sound Thomas had ever heard. He stared at the ceiling and tried to think as he tugged at his bonds. How could he get his hands untied? How could he get his ankles loose from the bedposts? How could he get out that door and past all the soldiers and down the street and all the way to Williamsburg?

The ceiling became a blur, and Thomas stopped pulling at the ties.

It's no use, he thought as his cheeks grew wet. *I hope Papa doesn't pay money to get me back, because I'm a failure!*

Before he knew it, he was crying hard, and before he was done, he'd fallen into an unhappy sleep.

Once his eyes jerked open to find Knox and Dickinson standing over him.

"He did it!" Knox was saying. "That stupid tobacco-picker tied him to the bed, just like we told him to."

"Of course," Dickinson explained patiently. "They're of a lower sort. They can only do what they're told."

Knox gave a high-pitched laugh. "Let's tell him to jump off the roof!"

Dickinson took off his hat and hit him with it.

No One isn't a lower sort! Thomas thought in a fog. *He's better than either of you!*

Thomas closed his eyes as they left. The next time someone came to the door, he didn't bother to open them.

This person didn't stomp loudly into the room jangling his sword. The door shut quietly behind him, and he seemed to float toward the bed. There was a muffled gasp, and Thomas was sure he heard the person say his name.

He did open his eyes then. They were crusty, and they hurt in the thin light that was creeping in through the window. But from what he could see, his visitor looked like a woman, holding a basket.

Well, our women help the Patriots, Thomas thought. *I guess the Loyalist women help the British.*

He suddenly thought of Betsy Taylor just now waking up in the room across from his at the homestead. *She wouldn't want to see me tied up like this, no matter whose side she's on,* he thought.

The lady at his bedside was wearing a strange kind of bonnet that nearly covered her face with its brim. She fumbled with the purse she had tied to her waist, and she pulled something out and reached for the cloth that held his left ankle to the bedpost. It was tiny knife!

With the skill of a carver, she cut his ankles free. Then she flipped him over and went to work on the ties around his wrists.

She's as strong as Malcolm! Thomas thought. *Have they hired her to take me to Papa?*

The woman pulled him back to face her and brought her lips close to his ear. Thomas tried to pull away, but the hand on his shoulder was like a vice.

"When I take the gag out of your mouth," she breathed into his ear, "don't make a sound."

With her gloved hands, the woman in the bonnet pulled the cloth out and tossed it behind her with a disgusted look.

"Animals," she whispered.

Thomas got himself up to his elbows and stared at her. *Was she on* his *side? If she was, how did she get in here?*

"We're going to have to move quickly," she whispered to him. Her voice was low, as if she had a sore throat. Thomas's heart began to slow down, and he looked at her curiously.

"Who are you—?" he started to say.

But the woman clapped her hand over his mouth and looked over her shoulder at the door. They stayed that way for at least half a minute before she looked back at Thomas.

"I told you, Thomas. Don't make a sound."

"But how did you know my name?" Thomas hissed.

This time she picked up a pillow and shoved it over his face. He grabbed at it, but she pushed harder, and Thomas stopped struggling. This was one strong woman.

Slowly, she peeled the corner of the pillow away and peeked under it. "You have a lot to learn about being a spy," she said in her low-pitched voice.

She pulled the rest of the pillow off and brought him up to her face by the shoulders. For the first time, Thomas saw under the wide brim of her bonnet. Round, brown eyes blinked down at him.

"Don't say it," whispered the "woman" above him.

So Thomas only mouthed the word: *Alexander!*

A dimple appeared in each cheek, and Alexander smiled the slice of a grin that was so much like Caroline's. "Do you like my dress?" he asked.

Thomas looked at the happy-pink gown and nodded numbly. He couldn't have spoken even if he'd been allowed to. His whole face was stunned.

"Good," Alexander whispered, "because I have one just like it for you here in my basket." He grinned again. "It's not quite as pretty, but I think you'll be perfectly fetching in it. Lucky for us they've already done away with your clothes."

With hands deft as a basket weaver's, Alexander opened the basket, produced a purplish-colored dress, and slung it over Thomas's head.

"Mistress Gibbons had quite a selection in her clothes press," Alexander whispered. "I chose this one because it has the matching bonnet."

While Thomas worked his arms into the sleeves, Alexander reached behind him and pulled out the string that held Thomas's dark hair into a tail at the base of his neck.

"Shake your head," he said.

Thomas did as was told, and he felt his unruly curls tossing everywhere. Alexander plopped a purple bonnet on top of them and tied it under Thomas's chin. He stepped back to look, and the grin sliced across his face.

"You look like a pomegranate," he said. "But don't speak and try not to trip over anything, and you should be fine." He picked up his basket and kicked at his skirts. "These create an extra hazard. It must be devilish hard being a woman."

He stopped whispering then and slipped to the door. Thomas started to follow, but Alexander put up his hand and listened at the crack. Then he beckoned him over. Thomas took one stride, stepped on the hem of the skirt, and sprawled headlong on the floor. Alexander snatched him up by the arm and listened tensely at the door. Thomas's heart was pounding again.

"I gave those two bumpkins downstairs some of my special bread," he said close to Thomas's ear. "Laced with sleeping powder. But I don't want to take a chance. Try not to make noise."

Thomas nodded. His mouth had gone dry, and his heart was working its way to his throat.

Alexander gave him a little nudge with his elbow. "I've found it helps if you hold the thing up with your hands—but not too far or they'll see your shoes." He snickered. "Mistress Gibbons didn't have any big enough for those feet."

Thomas snatched up his skirts with both hands and felt the sweat from his palms oozing through them.

Alexander gave a soft snort and pointed at the two figures slumped on the bottom step. Dickinson was snoring like a bull, and Knox slept with his head on Dickinson's chest, a trail of drool running down the front of his uniform.

"The British are certainly safe with these two on the watch," Alexander murmured. He jerked his head toward the dining room. "We'll go out that way," he said. "I've a buggy waiting at the side door."

This time Thomas didn't pause to think about when his family ate in that dining room. Hope was pumping through his heart now. *Maybe I* will *see them all again,* he thought.

Alexander straightened his bonnet and opened the door. As Thomas passed through, Alexander took his hand.

"You're my sister," he whispered. "You're too shy to talk or look at people." He snickered. "I would be, too, if I were a woman with hands that big."

Thomas was too nervous to glare at him. He just nodded and walked hand-in-hand with Alexander to a small, two-seated buggy that waited by the road. Thomas drew in his breath sharply, but Alexander poked him, and he bit his lip.

That's our *horse!* he wanted to say. *One of the ones the British stole that night!*

"What is this one's name?" Alexander whispered to him as they climbed into the buggy.

"Sam named him Patriot," Thomas whispered back. "But how did you—?"

"We can return him to his rightful home, along with you," Alexander said. "And tomorrow you can take this buggy back to the Fitzhughs." He shook his head, bonnet flapping. "I'd like to return all the goods these villains have stolen, but there isn't time for that." He clicked his tongue at Patriot, and the buggy began to move. "In fact, I only have time to take you to the edge of the plantation and then I must be on my way."

"But where—?"

"Whoa there, mistress!"

Alexander jerked his head up, and Thomas saw his knuckles go white around the reins. The captain was striding toward them from the direction of the Courthouse.

Alexander put his hand on his arm. "It's all right. Just look at your lap and stay quiet."

Thomas gripped the skirt with his sweaty-palmed hands and held his breath.

The captain strode up to the side of the buggy and leaned in. "Mistress," he said briskly.

"Yes, Captain?" Alexander said. His voice was light and smooth, almost like his mother's. "What is it? I must go. I have many deliveries to make today."

"Oh, you're not leaving, mistress," the captain said.

Thomas squeezed his dress to keep from bolting.

But Alexander didn't even flinch. "I beg your pardon, sir?" he said in his Betsy Taylor voice.

"Well, not without giving me a chance to thank you for your kindness to us. I've not tasted food that fine since I left London."

"Why, thank you, sir," Alexander said. "But I really must go and deliver more to the rest of the soldiers."

"You'll find most of them camped closer to Jamestown Ford," the captain said. He lowered his voice. "They're waiting for Lafayette. That little French Patriot sympathizer will get his comeuppance shortly, I warrant you."

"Well, I don't know anything about such matters, Captain

Rippon," Alexander said. Thomas was certain he was batting his eyelashes by now. "I only do what I can to help."

"And it looks as if *you* have help this time," the captain went on. "Who is this young lady? I didn't see her arrive with you."

Thomas squeezed his eyes shut. *Oh no!* he thought, his heart slamming. *We're caught now!*

"Of course you didn't," Alexander said gaily. "I only just fetched her from Mistress Plymell's house. She's been visiting there all summer. We thought the change would do her good—her being so shy and all."

"Is that what's the matter with her? Who is she? What's her name?"

"My, you are the curious one, aren't you, Captain?" Alexander said. "If you must know, she's my sister, Tabitha."

Thomas stiffened his neck to keep from looking up and glaring at Alexander.

"Big girl, isn't she?" Captain Rippon said.

Alexander gave a dainty gasp. "Really, Captain, you'll hurt her feelings!"

"Mistress, I hope I haven't offended you—"

"No, it's quite all right," Alexander said. Thomas felt the buggy lurch. "But I really must be on my way now."

"Of course. Please come back again, won't you?"

Alexander sniffed, and the buggy moved forward.

"Good-bye, mistress. Good day, Tabitha."

But Alexander didn't answer as he snapped the reins, and Patriot took off at a trot up Ballard Street.

Thomas sneaked a look back, but the captain had already turned away and was walking back toward the courthouse.

At least he isn't going right up to his room to find me

gone, Thomas thought. His insides were shaking like jellied preserves. His eyes flickered up to the second floor, to the window of the room he'd just been rescued from. There was someone there, looking down at the wagon.

Thomas tugged at Alexander's sleeve. "There's someone in my room!" he hissed.

Alexander didn't turn around. "Can you see who it is?"

Thomas squinted his eyes as the buggy continued to move him farther away. The head in the glass was round, and dark—and hairless.

"No One!" Thomas breathed out.

"I thought you said there was someone—"

"No. I mean it's No One! The slave boy! I hope they don't think he let me go!"

"Well, he helped," Alexander said.

Thomas turned to stare at him. "He did?"

"He found me fluttering around in the hall upstairs, and I told him I was looking for my son who was lost. He asked me if I were going to beat you if I found you. When I said no, he led me straight to you." Alexander looked at him sideways. "Is that your friend from Carter Ludwell's?"

Thomas nodded miserably. "Those soldiers will whip him worse than Carter ever did if they think he's the one who cut me loose."

Alexander shook his head. "They won't have a chance. Someone will be along shortly to take your friend up to Pennsylvania. There is a whole colony of slaves there that we've set free from the British. He'll be happy there."

Thomas didn't say anything. His thoughts were spinning at a dizzying pace.

It's absolutely true, then. Alexander is a spy for the

Patriots. I saw it with my own eyes and heard them talking—

Thomas bolted up, sending his bonnet off at a crooked angle.

"The captain was talking to someone outside the door last night!" he said. "They're trying to capture you, Alexander, and the commander is going to have you hanged!"

"I know," Alexander said mildly. "That's why I can take you only as far as the edge of the homestead. I've gotten away with as much as I'm going to around here. I had just finished my last message delivery last night when old Whiskers flagged me down." Alexander chuckled while Thomas gaped at him. "Look in the basket."

Thomas reached into the basket on the seat between them and pulled out a piece of paper. In the gray light of early morning, he saw his own face staring back at him, with a huge rag sticking out of it. On either side of him were Dickinson and Knox.

"Whiskers said they were taking you to the captain's headquarters, and I knew where that was." He smiled. "It's easy to get through as a woman. They have strict orders not to bother the ladies, especially if they provide the soldiers with baked goods. I've been there many times."

"Right under their noses!" Thomas cried.

Alexander nodded. "Those men are so busy putting on airs that they don't know what's happening right in front of them. That's why Captain Rippon didn't recognize your horse, or the buggy, even though it was he and his men who took them. They have taken so many things they don't even need that they don't know what they have."

Thomas leaned back against the seat and took a deep breath—perhaps the only easy breath he'd taken since before

Dawson Chorley had stormed up to the servants' porch last evening.

Was it only last evening? he thought to himself. *It seems like so long ago now.*

And then he sighed, not so easily this time. *And how are things any different now than they were then? I'm just as far away from Papa as I ever was. And Malcolm is no better off.*

"Those are heavy thoughts you're thinking, Master Hutchinson," Alexander said. "It's your new name you're worried about, eh? You don't like 'Tabitha'?"

He was grinning, but Thomas couldn't smile back. "I wish you could stay and help me get rid of Dawson Chorley," he said. "I can't do it alone."

Alexander's smile disappeared. "Is that the new overseer you tried to tell me about at the bridge that night?"

Thomas nodded miserably.

"I wish I could stay and help, too," Alexander said. "But suppose you tell me about it. Sometimes that can clear the head, eh?"

The miles between Yorktown and the homestead hurried by them as Thomas poured out the story. Alexander's frown grew deeper as he finished.

"What about your mama?" he said.

"She never knew. I don't think she could do anything about it anyway."

Alexander looked doubtful, but he shrugged. "I do know one thing, though, Thomas. You are not alone. You've prayed, of course."

"I've asked God over and over to please be a bridge between what we need and what I can do. But I don't see one, do you?"

Alexander slowed the buggy to a halt in a stand of trees

and began to untie his bonnet. "It's hard to say. But who knows? You may be standing at the very edge of it this minute and don't know it. Keep walking, Thomas—and keep praying." He pulled the pink dress over his head to reveal only his undershirt and drawers. He breathed a happy sigh. "I'm glad to be rid of that. Will you see to it that it goes to someone who can wear it with more grace?"

Thomas pushed the dress aside and leaned out of the buggy as Alexander jumped lightly to the ground. "Where will you go now?" he asked.

"I can't tell you that, Thomas. But I will say this—this war won't go on much longer. Especially after I deliver the word Captain Rippon just blurted out to me."

"About the surprise attack on Lafayette?"

Alexander nodded. "If I can get to the Patriot headquarters in time, there will be no surprise attack. I must go now."

Thomas only nodded. A sick wave had just washed over him, and he didn't trust himself to speak.

"God be with you," Alexander said softly. "And remember, don't tell a soul."

As he disappeared into the dawn, Thomas realized that once again, he hadn't asked him about Sam.

✝ ✦ ✝

Chapter Sixteen

Thomas sat in the buggy for a long time before the sick wave washed away and he could pick up the reins and coax Patriot out onto the road.

I'm a failure, Thomas thought as he let the horse plod slowly toward the house.

I've found no bridge at all.

He watched dismally as the mansion grew larger and larger before him.

I can't go in the front door like some honored guest, he thought. *I'll bring the buggy around back and slip in through the back door. Maybe, just maybe, they haven't discovered I was gone yet.*

Clinging to that little strand of hope, he drove the buggy to the back of the house and slipped the reins over the porch railing. So far no one seemed to be stirring.

Not even Dawson Chorley.

That thought sent a shiver up his spine, and Thomas had an uneasy rippling in his stomach as he hurried up the back steps and into the hall.

There was plenty of stirring there.

Mattie and Esther were standing beside the case clock, clinging to each other like a pair of abandoned kittens. A few of the other servants were clumped in the dining room doorway, faces pinched, and even Otis was lurking by the staircase, working his grizzled jaw. Above him, Patrick hung over the banister.

No one even looked up as he slipped in. Every eye was on the library door. From inside, Thomas heard Dawson Chorley.

"What does that prove? It's the scribbled imaginings of an arrogant boy! I won't be accused by his lying pen!"

"My son does not lie!" the other voice shouted back. "He is a Hutchinson! He has been raised in honesty!"

Mama!

Thomas gasped and heads turned his way. Esther moved to come for him, but Thomas held up his hand and stared at the library door.

"If you believe a word of what is written in the journal of that spoiled brat, then you, Mistress Hutchinson, have been raised in the dark!"

There was a short pause, and Mr. Chorley started in again with a lower voice. "Really, madam, I don't know why you came in here in the first place," he said, as if he were talking to a child. "There is nothing here in your husband's workplace that could possibly be of interest to you. I am looking after his business—"

"And doing a poor job of it from what I read here!" Mama cried. "This 'spoiled brat' as you call him has been breaking his heart trying to protect me from what I should have seen for myself. You are a brute, Mr. Chorley, and I will not have you on my property!"

There was a hard sound. Dawson Chorley was laughing.

"I see nothing amusing about this!" came Mama's voice. "You have committed heinous crimes here in a place that has known nothing but love and goodness since the day it was built."

"Heinous crimes!" the man roared. "Such as the night I saved that useless little servant girl you treat like a duchess? And pulled all your precious belongings off the British boat?" He gave an ugly snort. "I was unable to retrieve your silver candlesticks. Is that the heinous crime I am guilty of?"

There was a rustling of silk and paper, and then Mama's voice came out, low and menacing. "No, Mr. Chorley, your crimes are recorded in these pages that my son wrote, and I believe every word. He would never have left here in the dead of night without a word if he had not been desperate to find his father to come and make you pay for what you have done to the people here." There was another angry rustle. "I cannot make you pay, sir. Only my husband can exact what is due from your miserable hide. But I can demand that you leave this place at once."

"Thank the Lord!" Esther hissed, waving her fist in the air.

But from the library there came a cry—a pained one.

"He's hurting her!" Mattie cried.

Thomas charged to the door. It came open under his angry palms and banged against the wall. Dawson Chorley had taken hold of Mama's arm and had her pulled up to his face. He whirled to look behind him, and his mouth contorted in ugly surprise. Thomas jammed both fists into his ribs, and Dawson let go of Virginia Hutchinson and turned on him, snorting like an enraged bull.

"Beat me until I'm dead!" Thomas screamed in words he knew he'd heard before. "But don't you touch her!"

Dawson Chorley's chest heaved, and he kept his wooden club of a fist poised in the air. Thomas didn't move.

Chorley let out another of his hard laughs. "I beg your pardon, *Master* Thomas," he said, in a tone that sounded like spit. "But I find it hard to feel very threatened by a man who is wearing a dress."

Thomas felt his face burn, but he didn't drop his eyes. "I don't care if I'm stark naked," he said. "My mother told you to leave."

Mr. Chorley let his fist fall to his side, and his face tightened again. "I will go—for now," he said. "But I won't be far away. I want to hear what Master Hutchinson has to say when he returns and finds me gone." He gave Mama a sneering look. "I doubt he's the kind of man who allows his affairs to be managed by women and children."

He straightened his shoulders and marched from the room. Thomas heard a general scattering as he growled his farewell and slammed out the back door.

"Thomas!" Mama cried. She threw her arms around his neck, and for once he didn't pull away.

"You showed that monster, Thomas!" Esther called from behind them. "Just like I knew you could!"

Patrick, Mattie, and Esther gathered around them.

"I was frantic by this morning, wondering where you were," Mama said. "Mattie said you had been spending a lot of time in here, and that I might find some clue here. Betsy and Lydia helped me look, and we found your papers. We knew right away that you'd gone to fetch your father."

"We'd also gotten word by then," Esther put in, "that

those Redcoats were coming back this way. We were afraid you were right in the thick of it."

His mother stroked his hair. "When I sent for him, that wretched man stormed in here in a rage." She flashed her gray eyes. "I gave him a rage of my own."

"So we heard, mistress!" Esther said, cackling. "You both did us all proud!"

There was a round of head bobbing. Then faces began to look amused, and Patrick snickered.

"What is so funny?" Thomas asked.

"Well, you," Patrick said. "Wearing a dress. I especially like the bonnet."

Thomas snatched the purple hat from his head as the room erupted into laughter.

Mama shook her curls. "Why are you wearing a dress?"

How am I going to explain this without mentioning Alexander, Thomas thought uneasily. *I promised him I wouldn't tell his secret to anyone.*

"May I explain that later?" he said. "Right now, we have to get word to Papa."

"Word is already on its way," she said. "As soon as we found your papers, Betsy and Lydia insisted on taking the carriage and the girls and heading for Williamsburg themselves to tell your father. Betsy assured us that the British are under strict orders not to bother any women or children." Mama frowned. "I told her we hadn't found that to be true on their visit here, but she was determined, so I let them go."

"Cookie sent them with a basket of baked goods," said Mattie, "just in case they were questioned by any soldiers. "

Thomas's knees turned to jelly, and he sank into one of Papa's chairs. They *would* be all right, he knew. And they

would get the word to Papa, and Malcolm would be free and—
Malcolm!

Thomas sprang up from the chair again. "We have to get Malcolm out of the woodshed!" he cried. He hiked up his purple skirts and bolted from the library and out the back door with the others trailing behind him. He stopped dead on the top step.

Otis was moving slowly toward the servants' porch with Malcolm leaning heavily against him.

Skirt slapping at his ankles, Thomas ran to them and took Malcolm's other arm. The Scottish boy looked pale and tired, but he smiled his square smile until his eyes danced.

"You should wear dresses more often, lad," he said feebly. "They become you."

Thomas didn't even feel like punching him.

Esther made Malcolm lie down in the servants' hall. With Malcolm finally off to sleep, Thomas thought he would go out of his skin, waiting for word from Williamsburg.

"They must have gotten there by now!" he complained to Mama as she tried to get him to eat some dinner in the sitting room.

"I'm sure they have," she said, pushing a plate of cucumber salad toward him, "but it will take at least a few hours for Papa to get back here. Now please, Thomas, eat something." She smiled. "I never thought anyone would have to coax *you* to eat!"

Thomas nibbled halfheartedly on a slice of cucumber. Caroline was off in Williamsburg, fetching Papa back, and all he could do was sit here and eat lunch.

Maybe it's a good thing, though, he thought. *She'd make me tell about my adventure, and how would I get around Alexander?*

He was trying to imagine himself making up some other person to take Alexander's place in his story when his head nodded and his fork clattered to the plate.

"You're falling asleep, son," Mama said. "Why don't you lie down there on the lounge? I promise I'll wake you the minute I hear a word."

Thomas stumbled reluctantly to the lounge and sprawled out. "I'll rest," he said. "But I can't sleep."

Mama sat beside him and brushed his stubborn curves of hair off his forehead. "You know, you looked quite darling in that dress, but I want you to know that I would not trade my boy for any girl any time."

Thomas grunted—and then he was gone.

He woke up dripping with sweat in the middle of the afternoon. Mama was dozing in her chair, and Thomas slipped out and went down to the servants' hall. Malcolm was having the same argument with Esther that Thomas had had with his mother a few hours before.

"I can't sleep anymore, Esther!" Malcolm was wailing. "I've been locked up! I want to get out and move about!"

"Can't he come with me?" Thomas said. "I'll look after him."

Esther tapped her foot for a moment. "All right," she said finally, "as long as you do, Thomas."

"Let us get this straight right off, lad," Malcolm said as they went down the servants' porch steps. "I do not need any looking after."

"Then you'd better get out of everyone's sight," Thomas said, "because they all want to see to us like a bunch of mother hens."

"Malcolm! Thomas!" Patrick called from the stable. "I'm coming with you!" He trotted up to them, freckles all aflush. "Mattie says I'm to keep an eye on you both."

The two boys glared at him.

"Though I don't suppose you need much watching," Patrick added quickly.

"I say we go the bridge," Thomas said. "No one will bother us there."

There was a breeze kicking up off the river as the three made their way toward the cove. With the air moist and warm and the gulls squawking and the bank brilliant with wildflowers, Thomas felt more free than he had since the moment they'd first seen Dawson Chorley.

This is how I remember the plantation, he thought, his mind edged with a timid happiness. *No one should have to be afraid here, and they never will be again!*

"Let's fix up the bridge while I'm here, Patrick," he said. "We could really do a good job of it now."

"I know where we can get some good wood—" Patrick started to say.

But as they rounded the crest of the hill, he stopped and stared. Thomas halted beside him.

There in the cove where the bridge had stood was a pile of rubble, chopped into small pieces and lying broken on the bank. A few dismal pieces bobbed on top of the water.

"It must have been the storm yesterday," Patrick said.

But anger was burning up Thomas's backbone like a wildfire, and he could feel it blazing in his eyes.

"The storm didn't do that!" he said. "That was done with an ax."

"And it doesn't take much to guess whose," Malcolm said

tightly. He turned his head and spat into the grass.

Patrick stiffened until his arms stuck out at his sides. "I hate him!" he shouted. And then as if he'd been shot from a cannon, he exploded over the hill.

As he watched him go, Thomas started to say, "I hate Dawson Chorley, too."

But he couldn't.

Because he can't make me do things I don't want to do anymore, he thought. *I have too many people working to keep us all free together. We're like . . . well, we're all like a bridge that takes us to freedom.*

"We were going to rebuild it anyway," Thomas said.

Malcolm looked at him. "You don't want to go and knock him over the head with a musket barrel?"

Thomas shook his head. "You're the one who said we shouldn't hate," he said.

"So I did, lad," he said. "Let's go and see if Cookie has any fruit to suck on. I'm feeling a bit pale, eh?"

They meandered through the heat toward the house and were barely within sight of the back door when Thomas broke into a run.

"I'll meet you there, Malcolm," he called over his shoulder.

"Where are you going, lad?"

"To the house!" he cried. "Papa's there!"

And then he took off like a shot toward the speck on the back steps.

✢ ✦ ✢

Chapter Seventeen

For the first time since Thomas was a little boy, Papa picked him up and swung him around. Thomas hung on until his father set him back on the ground and searched his face with his deep-set Hutchinson eyes.

"It gave me a turn when Betsy Taylor and Lydia Clark appeared at my door this noon and told me you'd disappeared," he said. "And why you'd gone. They hoped you were already with me. When you weren't, they practically dragged me to the carriage and threw me in." He chuckled. "It took some doing to convince them that I could get here faster on Judge."

He pulled Thomas's face to his chest. "All I could do on the way to the homestead was pray that you would be here when I arrived."

"You aren't angry with me?" Thomas asked.

Papa held him at arm's length to look in his face.

"For what, Thomas? Trying to bridge the gap for me while I was gone? That only makes me proud, son." He turned to look over his shoulder as Mama joined them on the steps. "Though it looks as if your mother had as much to do with it, eh?"

Thomas grinned. "You should have heard her giving old Dawson Chorley what for."

"I'm sorry I missed that," John Hutchinson said. But his face clouded, and he moved to the bottom step as Malcolm reached it. "Let me help you," he said, offering his arm.

"I'm fine, sir," Malcolm said.

"Then let me offer you an apology," Papa said. "I was so blinded by what I saw as Dawson Chorley's bravery that I went against my better judgment and left him here in charge." His brow furrowed. "I was right to begin with. All of you are far more important than the supplies and belongings he saved."

Malcolm shook his head. "It's all right. It's all over now."

"Not quite," Papa said. "I will not rest until I have found that beast and turned him over to the proper authorities."

"He said he wouldn't be far away," Mama said.

Thomas nodded. "He didn't say where he was going, though."

Papa rubbed his chin. "He may have gone into Yorktown—"

"The town is full of British soldiers now," Thomas said.

Papa looked at him quizzically, and Thomas was afraid he was going to start asking him questions. But Papa wasn't ready to change the subject. "Then it's possible he went to Williamsburg, what with the British leaving there all of a sudden last night. But I would most likely have seen him if he'd been going that way."

Just then there was a hollering from across the yard that scattered the chickens in 17 squawking directions. Patrick charged toward them, red-faced and huffing.

"Thomas, Master Hutchinson!" he panted. "I saw him!"

"Saw who, Patrick?" Mama said.

"That . . . Mr. Chorley!" he said. He clutched at his sides to get his breath. "He has a tent pitched down by the river. He didn't see me, but I saw him—sittin' in front of it."

"Well, then," John Hutchinson said grimly. "I suppose you'd better point it out to me, eh?"

Papa started off across the yard.

"Papa?" Thomas called out. "May I come?"

His father looked back at him. "I didn't think there would be any stopping you."

"Where did he get that tent, I wonder?" Papa said as they peered down from the bluff at Dawson Chorley's little camp.

Thomas had seen the same kind of tent from the top of another hill not long ago. "That's a soldier's tent," he said.

Papa looked at him sideways. "You have covered a lot of territory of late, son. We must have a talk soon." Then he nodded thoughtfully. "He must have taken that off the boat the same night he collected our supplies from the British. There is no telling what he has in that tent."

Papa sighed and motioned for Thomas to follow him. They moved slowly down the hill and reached the clearing just as Mr. Chorley looked up.

"Mr. Hutchinson!" he said, using his happy-to-serve-you voice. "I didn't know when you'd return, sir. I wanted to discuss this situation with you as soon as—"

"There will be no discussion, Chorley," Papa said coldly. "Since you have not left my property as my wife instructed you to do, I have no choice but to ask you to come with me."

The big man drew himself up. "Sir, I was not told that I

was to take orders from the mistress."

"She is my wife and the head of the household in my absence. I would expect you to defer to her as well as to my son."

Mr. Chorley's eyes glittered over at Thomas. "Your *son*, sir," he said, in a voice he was trying hard to control, "has a tendency to stretch the truth somewhat, and your wife does not recognize that—"

"My wife," John Hutchinson cut in, "recognizes a snake in the grass when she sees one. And as for my son, he may be the most clear-seeing Hutchinson on this plantation. Now I will thank you to come with me quietly."

The servant's mask fell completely from Dawson Chorley's face. He clenched his tree bark hands at his sides. "Where would we be going, *sir?*" he said.

"To the proper authorities at the Yorktown Courthouse," Papa answered. "You have done serious physical harm to one of my servants and imprisoned him."

Thomas nudged his father's arm. "The British have taken over the courthouse in Yorktown, Papa," he said.

"Then I'll take you all the way to Williamsburg!" Papa burst out. "It makes no difference to me as long as I see you in a jail cell before sundown!"

"Arrogant brat!" Chorley cried.

It took Thomas a moment to realize Mr. Chorley was screaming at *him*. In that same moment, the big man sprang toward him and grabbed the front of Thomas's shirt.

But only for that moment.

The next moment, he was slammed against an oak tree— with John Hutchinson standing over him, chest heaving.

"I never strike a man," Papa said in a voice that was tense with all he held back. "I will not lower myself to your methods. But when you attack my son, you become an animal in my eyes—and then there is no limit to what I will do."

Dawson Chorley's eyes had rolled so far up into his head that all Thomas could see were the whites.

"Thomas, go into Mr. Chorley's tent and fetch him a clean shirt and stockings. He'll be going into town."

Thomas slipped into the tent with his head still reeling, though it slowed when he got inside. *What is all this?* he thought as he stepped over the piles of sacks that were stuffed in the tiny space. *Does he keep potatoes and flour?*

He spotted a few pieces of clothing in the corner and went toward them. His foot caught on one of the bags and struck something hard inside. Thomas bent down to pick up a linen shirt. But his eyes kept snagging on the bag he'd tripped on. Finally, he couldn't stand it. He pulled it open and peered inside.

"I just thought you might want to see this, Papa," Thomas said as he emerged from the tent.

Papa had just finished tying Mr. Chorley's hands behind him with the man's own rope belt when he looked up. His face froze.

"Are those—?"

"Yes, sir, they are," Thomas said as he held up the two tall pieces of silver. "They're Mama's candelabra."

There was a brilliant sunset the next evening. Thomas watched it from the back steps with Mama, Malcolm, Esther, and Otis while they all munched from the bowls of cherries that Mattie was passing around.

"Lydia and Betsy would be enjoying this," Mama said wistfully. "I know their leaving helped save the day for us, but I *am* sorry they're gone."

"You'll see them soon enough, I'm sure," Esther said, patting Mama's hand. "Good friends are never very far away."

It surely feels like Caroline and Patsy are far away, Thomas thought. Now that Dawson Chorley was gone, the homestead was a happy place again. A thousand times that day, he'd wished they were both with him so they could help him build the bridge again with Patrick . . . and feed apples to the horses . . . and watch this sunset. It was a palette of colors—reds and purples and oranges—all falling together like a pile of feathers.

"You've been watching that sky like a painter, Thomas Hutchinson," Mama said. "What do you see there?"

Thomas only had to think for a minute before he answered. "The Lord."

There was an awed silence as everyone looked.

"What is He doing?" Malcolm asked.

Thomas cocked his head. "I think He's building a bridge," he said, "for whoever needs it."

Patrick sailed around the side of the house just then, shouting, "He's coming! Master Hutchinson is coming!"

There was a general flurry through the house to the front door. Thomas nearly knocked Esther over wriggling to get out and down the road to meet his father. Judge thundered to a stop halfway up the drive, and his father leaned down and hauled him up. Thomas rode behind him to the front steps, hanging on and laughing for no reason that he could think of—except that he was happy.

After the hugs and greetings, Papa hushed everyone with his hand. "I have news," he said.

Malcolm's face lit up. "Dawson Chorley, sir?"

"In the jail, awaiting his trial next week," Papa said. "And it's packed with prisoners of war. He won't find a spot to lie down these next seven days."

"Lydia and Patsy?" Mama said. "And Betsy and Caroline?"

"Safely back in their homes. The British have left Williamsburg—and left it something of a mess, I might add."

"Where have they gone?" Thomas said.

"To fight Lafayette at Jamestown Ford," Papa said. His blue eyes twinkled. "Except that Lafayette never appeared. He received word that General Cornwallis was waiting for him, so he and his men stayed away."

Thanks to Alexander Taylor, Thomas thought happily. He could imagine Alexander nodding with satisfaction and then riding off to . . . wherever he was going next.

"Lafayette has settled just outside Williamsburg with his troops, waiting for General Washington perhaps to send him more. As for General Cornwallis, he has decided to settle in Yorktown and wait to fight the Patriots there."

"Fight in Yorktown!" Mama cried.

"A stone's throw from here, my dear," John Hutchinson said. "That is why I must send you all back to Williamsburg— you, Thomas, Malcolm, Esther, and Otis. I will stay and make arrangements for the servants should it become too dangerous here. And I must oversee the plantation until I find someone suitable." He looked at Thomas. "Or until our son grows just a little older and can do the job himself."

Thomas stared.

"You shouldn't be surprised, Thomas," Papa said. "That smart little Caroline said it. You are a clear-seeing man. A clear-eyed Hutchinson man."

✢·✦·✢

Chapter Eighteen

"Tom, I don't see why you won't tell *me*," Caroline said. "I'm still your best friend, aren't I?" She stopped wiping the apothecary shop window with the rag. "You didn't make Patrick your best friend while I was gone from the plantation, did you?"

Thomas looked up from the bottle of ginseng he was wrapping for Mistress Wetherburn and sighed. "No, you're still my best friend," he said wearily. "I've told you a hundred times."

"Then why won't you tell me what happened that night when you went looking for your father? Why did you come back in a dress?" Her brown eyes danced. "Malcolm says Patrick found *another* dress under the seat of the Fitzhughs' buggy when you brought it back. And how did you end up with their buggy anyway?"

Thomas silently wrapped some twine around the package.

Caroline crossed the shop and leaned over the counter. "I bet you looked awfully pretty in that purple dress, Tom."

"I looked like a pomegranate," Thomas told her flatly. "Now leave me alone."

"Not until you tell me."

Thomas chewed the inside of his mouth. They had been through this at least a dozen times in the month he had been back from the plantation, and every time it had been worse than the one conversation with his father. At least Papa had let him simply assure him that he hadn't done anything wrong and let it go at that. But Caroline was relentless.

"I wish your mama hadn't given those clothes away to Mattie," she was wheedling now. "I would have liked to have seen you in at least that bonnet."

"No!" Thomas cried.

"Hutchinson!" a voice wheezed from the examination room behind them. "Are you visiting or working?"

"Working, sir!" Thomas said at once—and shot Caroline a warning look.

"You haven't heard the last of this, Tom," she said between her teeth.

Old Francis Pickering walked stiffly into the room, carrying a basket of newly dried herbs from the cellar and wiping the sweat from his half-bald head with a handkerchief. He peered over his spectacles at Thomas.

"It's a good thing," the old man said. "After bein' wiped out by those lousy British, it's like startin' all over again around here."

"I'll take this to Mistress Wetherburn for you now, if you like," Thomas said, picking up the package of ginseng.

"No need to do that. I'm on my way to the Wetherburns myself."

Thomas looked up and smiled at Dr. Nicholas Quincy,

whose lanky form barely darkened the front doorway as he came in.

"Is that woman still hysterical?" Francis said from behind the counter. "The British have been gone for a month, and she's still lyin' abed with the shakes."

Caroline grinned her slice of a smile. "She just likes to have Dr. Quincy come and see her," she said mischievously.

Nicholas Quincy turned red and ducked his head. Francis gave a grunt and began to grind some licorice root, though his lips were twitching. Caroline reached into a jar and helped herself to a cinnamon drop and sucked on it while she watched Thomas pick up his broom and start to sweep.

Suddenly, the smells of the shop surrounded him like a pair of warm hands, and Thomas smiled to himself. It felt good to be back here in the shop with his friends around him. Everything was comfortable and familiar, even as every day the war changed it in some way.

Sam was gone, and Clayton, and Alexander. And now, of course, No One.

Papa was at the homestead almost all the time.

And the town was crowded once again with fearful plantation folks who had fled to Williamsburg for safety from the British in Yorktown.

But there were good things, too, Thomas decided as he swept.

Mama was running their house in Williamsburg much differently now. The place was always humming with women gathering to make bandages and to pray together, and little girls coming for needlework lessons. At least once a week she had army officers in for dinner: New Englanders, Jerseymen, Pennsylvanians, and Virginians who were serving under

Lafayette. And at last she had told Esther she was only to be her companion from now on—and she had hired a new cook, whose potato balls were almost as good as Cookie's. There didn't seem to be a problem she couldn't see to.

Still, Thomas missed the plantation—Mattie and Patrick and the sunsets and the new bridge they'd only gotten halfway built. And his room in the Williamsburg house seemed small and cramped after the spacious one at the homestead mansion.

But no sick wave washed over him whenever he thought about it. That was home, yes, but this was home, too. He remembered now how Papa had explained it to him just before he'd left the homestead. They'd been sitting in the library, sharing a dish of licorice drops, and Papa had watched him closely for a long time.

"This is a different boy that I see before me," Papa had said finally. "Much different from the boy I sent off to Williamsburg last time."

"Everyone says that," Thomas said. "I know I'm taller, but—"

"There are other ways to grow. Think about Clayton, how sure and peaceful he was the day he left for England. Little Patsy. She wouldn't speak to anyone when she first came here. Now I can hardly keep her off my lap!" He selected another licorice drop. "And your mother—she's changed most of all. There was a time when she could barely stir her own tea. Now she's standing up to the likes of Dawson Chorley!"

"How have I changed?" Thomas asked.

"Let me just tell you the most important change I see. You have learned to like Thomas Hutchinson as he is . . . and to let God bridge the gap between that and everything else. Now you can be at home anywhere, in any situation—no matter who you may or may not have with you."

"Do you suppose that's why I'm not as sad to leave the plantation as I thought I would be?" he asked.

Papa had nodded and said, "That doesn't mean you won't miss things, as I will miss you. But you'll keep it all in your heart, eh?"

He was jerked from his thoughts by Francis's wheezing voice, calling, "Are you going to stand there smilin', boy, or are you going to sweep that floor and see to washing those jars like I told you?"

Thomas jumped. "Yes, sir, sweep, sir!"

Caroline headed for the door. "I must go home," she said. "Mama says I have to work on my sampler this afternoon or I'll never get a husband."

She wrinkled her nose and left.

Thomas watched her skip past the glass, and his heart made the only dip it ever did these days. That was when he thought about Alexander and the promise he had made to him. It was hard to keep a secret like that from Caroline.

"Sweep, Hutchinson!" Francis barked.

Williamsburg was starting into its evening cool as Thomas walked home from the apothecary shop that night. Fireflies were winking one by one, and the greens of the trees deepened in the fading light. Thomas was turning the corner to go up the Palace Green toward his house when the bell of the town crier clanged from the Market Square.

Doors flew open and windows were thrown up. People poured out of the taverns and shops until the Duke of Gloucester Street was thronged with folks, craning their necks to see the crier who hurried to stand at the top of the

Courthouse steps to be heard.

"Hear ye! Hear ye!" he shouted. "The French Admiral de Grasse has arrived on the Chesapeake Bay from the French West Indies with 28 ships carrying three French regiments!"

He repeated his message, and the people chattered among themselves.

Thomas stood on tiptoes and strained to hear more. Someone poked him in the side.

"Did you hear that, lad?" Malcolm said.

"I did, but—"

"The French are hemming old Cornwallis in from the sea!" Malcolm's dark eyes shone. "That means Lafayette can close in from land, if he gets more men. The war could be won right there in Yorktown!"

"There are 7,500 British soldiers camped around Yorktown now, boy," a man said at Malcolm's elbow. "Lafayette and the others barely have 3,000!"

He moved away, and Malcolm rolled his eyes. "Some people have no faith, eh, lad?" he said. "What is it you always say, 'God will build a bridge between what we need and what we have'?"

"Hear ye! Hear ye!" the crier called again. "British troops at Yorktown are digging trenches and building walls, preparing for battle!"

A deep moan rippled through the crowd.

"I don't know what they're worried about," Malcolm said to Thomas. "I tell you, this could win the war for us!" He gave Thomas's shoulder a squeeze. "I'm goin' to hang about for a bit and see what the soldiers are sayin'."

Thomas watched as Malcolm was swallowed up by the anxious press of people and then wriggled his way out and onto the Palace Green.

This is exciting, he thought. *A battle so close and perhaps a victory. More soldiers coming to town, maybe even Sam.*

His steps slowed as he thought of his brother. If only he could just know if he were safe.

"Tom!" someone called to him from the other end of the Green. It was Caroline, and she ran toward him with her hair flying free behind her. As she drew closer, Thomas could see that her face was alive with an idea.

"All right, Tom!" she said when she reached him. "Here is how I will do it."

"Do what?" Thomas said. He could feel his eyes narrowing.

"Get you to tell me the story of your adventure in Yorktown!"

Thomas groaned.

"It will be a game!" she said, tossing her hair. "Walk with me."

He let her tug him to his yard along the Green and pull him down beside her against a willow by the fence.

"All right," she said. "I will ask you only questions that you can answer yes or no to."

"Caroline—"

"Please, Tom?"

Her voice caught, and for an awful moment, Thomas thought she was going to cry. All along he'd thought she wanted to hear the story because she hated being left out of an adventure. But it sounded as if this were really important to her.

"All right," he said slowly. "But I might not answer all of them."

"Yes, you will," she said. Her voice took on its lilt again, and she began. "Did you, in fact, go to Yorktown that night?"

Thomas sighed.

"Did you?"

"Yes!"

"Good. Now then, did soldiers take you there? Did they capture you?"

"That's two questions!"

"Answer them!"

"Yes—and yes."

"Did you see Sam there?"

"No. I wish I had!"

"Did you see Alexander? Is he safe?"

"I didn't say—"

"Please, Tom," she said. Her voice quavered softly. "He's my brother."

My brother, Thomas thought. *What I wouldn't give to know that my brother was safe. But I promised! Oh, God, I need another bridge!*

"Is he alive—and free?" she asked.

Thomas took a deep breath. His heart was pounding.

"Yes and yes. But please, Caroline, don't ask me any more questions."

"I don't *have* any more questions," she said. She grabbed his hand. "Come on, let's go catch some fireflies."

"Where?" he said as he scrambled after her.

"Why don't we see if there is anyone on the Chinese Bridge, behind the Governor's Palace?" she said.

Thomas grinned and followed her. Right then he couldn't think of a more perfect place to be than a bridge.

✦ ✦ ✦